"Come here, Angel," Nicholas said, wrapping his fingers around her arm.

"I have to leave so you can rest."

"Angels give aid and service to the sick and suffering, don't they? Well, I'm both. Give aid and service to me, Angel."

"I'm not an angel."

"I'm beginning to believe you're *my* angel."

She pressed her free hand against his chest. "Nicholas—"

"I know," he muttered. "I know all the reasons why I shouldn't do this. But I'm going to have to do it anyway." He curved his other hand around her neck and pulled her down until his lips crushed hers.

The need to kiss her was overwhelming, tightening his gut, hardening his muscles, firing his blood. He heard her moan softly. A man could find ecstasy with her. Paradise.

But he knew it couldn't be. Paradise wasn't for him—there was too much guilt, too much bitterness and grief in him. But surely he could kiss her for just a bit longer. . . .

Angel was breathless beneath the onslaught of Nicholas's kiss. She never should have allowed him to teach her that kisses could be so addictive, so hot. She shouldn't have wanted him so badly.

"Angel—" He let his hands drop away from her, and she pushed away from him until she was sitting up.

"Whatever you do, Nicholas, don't you dare say you're sorry. . . ."

WHAT ARE *LOVESWEPT* ROMANCES?

They are stories of true romance and touching emotion. We believe those two very important ingredients are constants in our highly sensual and very believable stories in the *LOVESWEPT* line. Our goal is to give you, the reader, stories of consistently high quality that may sometimes make you laugh, sometimes make you cry, but are always fresh and creative and contain many delightful surprises within their pages.

Most romance fans read an enormous number of books. Those they truly love, they keep. Others may be traded with friends and soon forgotten. We hope that each *LOVESWEPT* romance will be a treasure—a "keeper." We will always try to publish

LOVE STORIES YOU'LL NEVER FORGET
BY AUTHORS YOU'LL ALWAYS REMEMBER

The Editors

Fayrene Preston

Satan's Angel

BANTAM BOOKS
NEW YORK · TORONTO · LONDON · SYDNEY · AUCKLAND

SATAN'S ANGEL

A Bantam Book / December 1991

If you would be interested in receiving protective vinyl
covers for your Loveswept books, please write to this address
for information:

Loveswept
Bantam Books
P.O. Box 985
Hicksville, NY 11802

ISBN 0-553-44169-8

Published simultaneously in the United States and Canada

PRINTED IN THE UNITED STATES OF AMERICA

OPM   0 9 8 7 6 5 4 3 2 1

To Frances Perine,
an honest and wickedly funny angel
who's always told us how it is.

One

He was lost. Somewhere along the way he had taken a wrong turn. He rubbed his eyes and felt the grit behind his lids. When had he last slept? He couldn't recall. Nights and days had begun to run into one another until he couldn't tell them apart and didn't much care if he did or not.

He should probably pull over and look at the map, he thought wearily, but he didn't want to stop. The speed at which he drove kept the pain partially at a distance. Unfortunately, the car wasn't capable of the blinding, numbing, silver-streaking speed he needed to completely obliterate the pain emanating from his heart and searing his marrow. And in reality going twice or even three times the speed of sound probably wouldn't work anyway.

He jammed a Rolling Stones tape into the cassette deck, cranked up the volume, and pressed his foot down on the accelerator. He was heading south along a lonely stretch of Oregon road with the ocean and the setting sun to his right. If he weren't so tired, maybe he could figure out how to get back onto the main road. If he weren't so tired . . .

Suddenly, the road curved out so that it looked as if he were driving directly into the ocean and the setting sun.

The sun was a great, dazzling golden ball, hanging in the sky before his eyes, tipping the waves of the ocean with gilt and luring him with its brilliance. A powerful urge seized him to ignore the next curve in the road and to keep going on, straight toward the ocean, toward the sun. There would be no more pain, no more weariness, no more responsibility for anything.

A vision appeared in front of him. A woman with long blond hair, dressed all in white. The sun backlighted her, illuminating her with a breathtaking radiance. And fluttering out behind her were . . . wings.

"An angel," he whispered, stunned.

And he was about to hit her.

He jerked the wheel and slammed on the brakes, sending the car into a spin. The world whirled before his eyes. Trees, ocean, sky, angel, all blurred as he fought to regain control. He should be able to stop, he thought, bewildered. It should be so simple. But the lightning-quick reflexes and natural strength he had always taken for granted had deserted him.

He was about to die.

He heard a horrendous crash, metal crunching, glass shattering, a scream. And then darkness.

* * *

Pain was like a knife in his skull. He couldn't move. His entire body throbbed and ached. He was in hell, he thought without surprise. He had earned it.

Something whispered nearby, something fluttered. How odd.

His eyelids felt as if they were weighted by lead, and he was content not to see. He heard himself moan, and reflected on the uselessness of the effort. There would be no ceasing of his agony, he knew. It would go on and on for all eternity.

There was a gentle murmuring, a whiff of a light, fragrant scent, a tender, soothing touch. Curiosity reached past the pain, and slowly he forced his eyes open.

An angel stared down at him, the angel he had seen before.

He closed his eyes for a moment, then opened them again. She was a dreamlike vision. Her blond hair fell in silky waves past her shoulders and down over her breasts. Her skin was very fair, almost translucent, and flawless. Her eyes were the clear, startling blue of the sky he had often seen as he raced above the clouds, flying high above the earth. Light surrounded her. And behind her he could see . . . more angels.

Something was wrong. Hell didn't have angels.

"Where am I?" he asked, his voice little more than a thick whisper.

"You're in Paradise."

He almost believed her. Her voice was sweetly

musical, and her lips looked as if they were incapable of a lie.

"Can you tell me your name?" she asked.

Of course he could, he thought crossly. "Satan."

One pale brow lifted slightly. "Satan? Are you sure?"

"Yes." He was confused about a lot of things, but not his name. Did angels have names? he wondered.

"I'm Angel."

She was incredibly lovely—the thought came to him through the pounding pain. She deserved a name, not just an identity. But then again, Angel seemed very right for her. A beautiful, ethereal being who was not of the earth.

"You crashed," she said. "You were driving too fast and lost control of your car."

"Speeding is just one of my sins." He had so many, he didn't know where or how to start listing them.

"You're going to be all right," she said softly. "I don't want you to worry. I'm going to take care of you."

He couldn't tear his gaze away from her. She was the one light in the otherwise utter darkness. He should tell her, he thought. She should know that somehow a mistake had been made and he had ended up in the wrong place. "Satan doesn't belong in paradise. He fell from heaven."

She looked at him with concern, then turned and gazed into the darkness. "He's not making sense. I think he's hurt worse than we thought."

A deep, booming, godlike voice answered her. "Some disorientation is natural. Just keep an eye on him. You know where I'll be if you need me. If necessary, we'll call for an ambulance and take him to the hospital. But it'll be easier on him if we can spare him that sixty-mile trip."

"No." His reaction was strong and immediate. He'd spent too much time in hospitals lately, seen too much suffering.

Her hand smoothed across his brow. "Shhh. It's all right. You won't have to go to the hospital. I'm going to keep you here with me. I'm going to watch over you."

Her touch calmed him; her gaze reassured him. "Good," he mumbled, letting his eyes drift closed. "Good."

He was too tired, too hurt, to question how the miracle of her had happened to him. But for now, at least, an incredibly beautiful angel was going to watch over him.

Dreams mingled with the pain in his head and made his sleep fitful. He heard the explosions again, saw the balls of fire light up the sky, heard the screams. Anguish cut through him, tears ran down his face, and he cried out, "I'm sorry! I'm so sorry."

He felt her hand on his face, soothing, compassionate, healing. He quieted.

Angel continued to stroke his brow and face, careful to avoid the bandaged wound just above his left temple where he had hit his head in the crash. Her touch seemed to ease him in some way, as if he wasn't used to gentleness but craved it.

She studied him, inexplicably compelled. He was

in his thirties, she judged and she knew his eyes were midnight black from when he had awakened and gazed up at her. He had strong features that were even and well formed, with a jawline that looked as if it had been carved out of stone. His hair was thick, black, and styled short. His nose was straight, and his lips were full and firm and with a sensual shape that disturbed her on some deep, puzzling level.

What was a man like him doing in Paradise? A man who drove a frightfully expensive car and wore an elegant, custom-tailored suit. A man tortured by something so strong it wouldn't let him rest. A man who called himself Satan.

His night's growth of beard felt scratchy beneath her hands, tickling her palm and bringing all her womanly instincts rushing to the surface of her consciousness, womanly instincts that had more to do with sexuality than nurturing. She frowned, puzzled at her reaction to him. Noting that his breathing was deep and even now, she reluctantly pushed herself up from the bed.

As she walked into the kitchen, she pondered her unwillingness to leave him. It made no sense. Nor did this sudden activation of all her senses. She reached for the coffeepot, poured herself a cup, and decided on the spot that she couldn't possibly be attracted to a total stranger.

No. These unfamiliar feelings were due exclusively to the fact that she had been badly shaken. After all, she had walked directly into his path and been seconds away from death. His quick reflexes had saved her life, and he had harmed himself in the process. She owed it to him to take care of him.

She'd had a crush on her English teacher when she had been fifteen, her math teacher when she was sixteen. She had dated the high school football captain when she was seventeen. She could name a dozen or more movie stars, even more acquaintances, who she thought were great-looking.

But racing pulses weren't for her. Until now.

Satan. It was obviously a nickname, she reflected, sipping the coffee. She and Matthew had checked his billfold for identification. They had found a platinum American Express card in the name of Nicholas Santini, and six hundred dollars in cash. But there had been no pictures and no number to contact in case of emergency. His driver's license had also stated that his name was Nicholas Santini, and had listed an address in California.

How did a man earn the nickname of Satan? she wondered.

"I can't do it! I can't go up again!"

The anguish in his voice jolted her. She quickly put down the cup and hurried back into the bedroom. He was tossing and turning and had kicked the covers to the end of the bed.

"There, there," she murmured, coming down beside him, leaning over him, and gripping his upper arms. He thrashed on the bed as if he were fighting against some inner demon. She laid her upper body across him, trying to still him. Sweat sheened his skin, and his muscles rippled as he continued to try to toss about. His masculinity was almost overwhelming, but she couldn't let herself think about it. "Everything's going to be all right," she crooned. "Do you hear me? Everything's going to be all right."

"He lost it," he muttered. "Oh, Lord, he's going to crash!"

There was an intense sorrow and a profound grief in his voice, but he wasn't talking about himself. Something or someone had deeply wounded him, and she wished she knew what it was so she could help him. He seemed so vulnerable, and her heart ached for him.

"You're going to be all right," she whispered near his ear. "I'm going to see to it that you get better."

The tension eased from his body, and he turned his head slightly toward her mouth.

He had heard her. With a smile she lifted her body from his and caressed his brow. "I'm here with you, and I'm going to take care of you."

When she was sure that his bad spell had passed, she released his arm, but before she pulled the covers up, some deeply seated, purely feminine impulse propelled her to take a look at all of him. Matthew had undressed him down to his briefs, and warmth crept beneath her skin as she looked her fill. He was tall and lean with hard muscles layered beneath smooth bronze skin. Dark purple bruises had already appeared down the length of his left side. Fine, silky black hair covered his broad chest and narrowed to disappear beneath his briefs. He was an athlete with a virility that made the breath catch in her throat, and she was helpless to prevent her response. Her eyes returned to his briefs and the tantalizing bulge there. This man was affecting her in ways she wasn't used to. He was asleep now. How would she handle it when he woke up? she wondered warily.

She lifted one of his hands and ran her fingers along the calluses she found. A man of action, and judging by his clothes and car, a man used to the finer things in life. He was certainly out of his element here in Paradise, she reflected wryly, and turned her attention to his fingers. They were long with well-manicured nails. He wore no rings, and there was no ridge on the third finger of his left hand where a wedding band might have been.

As she pulled the covers over him, she glanced at the clock. Matthew had told her to wake him every so often, and if she couldn't, to call him immediately.

"I'm sorry," he mumbled, rolling his head from side to side. "It's my fault."

He blamed himself for something. Whatever it was, he seemed to be punishing himself as no man should, and it hurt her to watch. She repaired broken things for a living. He made her want to repair him.

She grasped his arms. "Nicholas, wake up."

He heard her voice, soft and melodic, pulling at him, tugging him from the dark pit where he had been.

She shook him lightly. "Nicholas. Open your eyes and look at me so I'll know you're all right."

He could never deny that voice, he thought. That voice could reach him in hell. Profoundly relieved that he was no longer dreaming, he did as she asked.

As before, light surrounded her, shining on her blond hair and giving her an unearthly radiance.

Angels flanked her shoulders. He ran his tongue over dry lips. "Thank you."

"For what?"

"For being here."

She smiled at him. "I'm glad that I'm helping."

He stared at her, his black eyes startling her with their intensity. "You're very brave to come into hell after me. Your wings could catch on fire."

Her smile faded, and she leaned forward to lay the back of her hand against his face. His skin was cool. "How are you feeling?"

Her hair brushed against his chest, and her light, airy fragrance settled around him. "You smell wonderful."

Concern showed in the way her brows drew together. "Are you in a lot of pain?"

Her eyes were endlessly blue, and just for a moment he thought he could see heaven. "My head is pounding, and my body feels as if it's been through a meat grinder."

"Unfortunately, you're going to hurt for a while. You hit your head really hard."

She straightened away from him as if she were about to get up, but he reached out and grabbed her hand, determined to keep her by his side. He would be plunged into darkness again if she left.

"What's wrong? Is there something you want me to do for you?"

"Yes," he said softly but decisively. "Stay with me. Don't leave me."

"All right," she said, moved by his request and the fear that had prompted it. "I'll sit in the chair over there." She pointed toward the shadows.

"*No.*" Pain showed on his face as he tried to focus

on her. "I don't know what you're doing here, but when you're near, I don't dream."

His need for her roused emotions she couldn't comprehend. He called himself Satan, and something terrible was eating him up inside. He was trouble with a capital T, but if he wanted her to stay by him, then she was going to stay. "If you think it will help, I'll sit here for a while."

"It will." His lids slowly closed, and he drifted off to sleep. But his hand remained clasped around hers.

She glanced at the clock. One A.M. She was tired, but she didn't dare sleep. Thankfully, his breathing seemed normal and his skin remained cool. She thought longingly of her coffee, and after thirty minutes had passed, she eased his hand from hers and got up. She was in the kitchen, pouring herself a new cup, when she heard him cry out.

She rushed back to his side. Smoothing her hand over his face, she crooned to him until he was quiet again. In his bedeviled sleep he reached for her hand.

She spent the next hour watching him, wondering what had brought him to that curve in the road, what tormented him so. Whatever the answers, he had crashed to avoid her, and she was grateful. Even so, no matter what she had decided before, she didn't think this instinctive urge to comfort and heal him stemmed entirely from gratitude.

"Nicholas, wake up. Wake up."
He heard her voice, and once again did as she

asked. Intense relief washed through him at the sight of her still beside him, watching over him. She lighted the darkness surrounding him. "Hello."

She smiled down at him. "It's around three-thirty in the morning. How are you doing?"

"Fine. I wasn't dreaming." He moistened his lips with his tongue.

She noted the action and reached for the glass of water she had placed on the nightstand. "Try to take a drink." Sitting on his right side, she slipped an arm beneath him, lifted him slightly, and placed the glass to his mouth.

Her hair brushed the side of his face, and her breast pressed against his arm. A thin stream of heat twisted and coiled through his insides. Turning his head slightly so he could see her, he took several swallows of water.

He wanted an angel. What was wrong with him? Heavenly, ethereal beings didn't feel passion and desire. A man couldn't take one into his arms and kiss her until both his and her blood ran hot. He couldn't caress her until a fire burned in his belly and his body hardened.

So, having clarified the matter, *why* did he still want her?

She replaced the glass on the table and eased him back to the pillow. "Better?"

"Yes." His head whirled and throbbed, his body ached, but he kept his eyes on her. She was important. "You're the angel I saw right before I crashed."

Her lips curved with amusement. "I'm not an angel. My name is Angel."

"I almost ran over you."

"I know, and I'm really sorry. You crashed because of me. I would never have started out into the road if I'd known you were coming. But you were driving so fast, you were nearly on top of me before I knew it."

He frowned, trying to remember something he was sure he was supposed to know. "Where did you say I was?"

"Paradise." She pressed the back of her hand to his cheek to check for fever. "Oregon."

What she was saying didn't quite make sense, he thought.

"Where were you going?" she asked quietly.

He reflected for a minute on her question. "Away, just away." He caught her hand and brought it down until it rested on his chest. Her hand was small and delicate in his, but holding it comforted him, and while he held it, she couldn't leave him. "I was certain I would wake up in hell."

"Your crash was about as bad as they come," she said solemnly. "I can see why you thought you were going to die."

"I'm still not sure I didn't."

Beneath her hand his heart beat strongly. "I'm happy to say you're alive. Trust me, you're going to be fine."

"I trust you," he said without stopping to think why he did. "But I don't understand."

"What don't you understand?"

"What are you doing here?"

"I live here," she said, wondering if she had been too quick to proclaim his recovery. Was he still suffering from disorientation?

He stared at her for a moment. "I didn't know there were angels on earth."

She frowned. "I told you, I'm *not* an angel. My *name* is Angel."

"If you're not an angel, then why do you look so much like one? And why are you surrounded by light? And why do you have angels behind you?"

Startled, she glanced over her shoulder, then smiled. "There's a floor lamp behind me—that must be the light you're seeing. And I have a collection of porcelain angels. Part of them are on a shelf in back of me."

"You're not an angel?"

She shook her head.

"I'm not sure I believe that."

She gave a light, golden-toned laugh. "Believe me."

He did and he didn't. He had never seen an angel before, even those times when he had flown his jet straight up toward heaven. On the other hand, he couldn't get it out of his mind that she wasn't of this earth.

She pulled her hand from his and patted his chest. "Go back to sleep."

"Not yet," he muttered. "Not until I find out for sure if you're flesh and blood."

He pulled her down to him and fastened his lips to hers. Taken completely by surprise, she went rigid, and her heart slammed wildly against her rib cage.

"You taste like heaven," he muttered, and increased the pressure of the kiss until she opened her mouth and allowed his tongue entry. It was like dipping into a honey vat, he thought with a shudder, and closed his arms around her.

She went limp against him. His kiss was overtaking her, inducing responses she couldn't control. His tongue was exploring and expert, his hands on her back strong and demanding. Feelings were awakening in her, but they were totally inappropriate feelings. And this was wrong. He was a man who had been hurt because of her; she was supposed to be taking care of him, not making love to him.

"We've got to stop," she managed, levering herself away from him.

"No." He still didn't know if she was angel or woman, but he couldn't let her go. He pulled her back down to him, crushing her breasts against the solid wall of his chest.

"You've been hurt," she said breathlessly.

His eyes were as dark as the night sky when he caught her face in his hands and gazed up at her. "Kissing you makes me feel better, and the hurt almost goes away."

"You're upset. You don't know what you're doing."

"Whatever you say." He stroked her throat with the tips of his fingers, leaving a trail of heat, then claimed her mouth once again and proceeded to teach her lessons about kissing. She hadn't known a mere kiss could seduce or inflame or turn her will to jelly. She hadn't known there were so many nerve endings in her lips or that the rasp of his tongue against hers could make her quiver. She hadn't known a kiss could bring her alive and make her want what she had never had before. She hadn't known . . .

Gradually, his arms relaxed their hold, and the pressure of the kiss eased. His strength was giving out, she realized, feeling a stab of disappointment that shocked her. Fine tremors radiated through her, hindering her ability to pull away quickly from him.

When she had straightened, he lifted a hand and touched her cheek. "I believe you." His voice was husky, rough.

"About what?" she asked, confused by the heat that lingered in her.

"I'm in paradise." He closed his eyes and slowly drifted back to sleep.

Before dawn she wakened him twice more. Each time she asked him his name. Each time he said Satan. Each time she offered him water, and after drinking, he fell asleep again. He was a strong man, she thought as she watched him sleep, a tormented man. A man who had set fire to her blood with a kiss.

He had been disoriented. It was the only answer.

He wouldn't remember what had happened between them in the morning. She, on the other hand, would probably never forget.

Two

He remembered everything.

He remembered how every time he had opened his eyes in the night, she had been there. He remembered how she had calmed him with her touch, and how soft and desirable she had felt in his arms. He remembered how she had said she wasn't an angel, but then had proceeded to make him feel as no earthly woman ever had—strangely peaceful, oddly feverish, and agonizingly needy. Despite his throbbing pain he had wanted her, and if his strength hadn't given out, he would have tried to bury his body in hers and find out for sure if he was in heaven or if he was in hell.

Now it was morning, and she wasn't in the room.

He would know if she was, he thought. He would hear her as she fluttered quietly around him. He would smell her light fragrance. He would feel the brush of her hand on his brow, the warmth of her palm on his cheek.

She wasn't in the room, and he felt a vague sting of dissatisfaction.

Slowly, he opened his eyes. His head no longer seemed as if it were going to come apart, but a dull, forceful ache did remain, and a light hurt had settled in his body, particularly on his left side.

He remembered how he had demanded that she sit beside him while he slept. Whatever the reason, he had let down his guard with her, had let her see him as no one ever had, and had turned his well-being over to her. He had trusted her, and in turn she had whispered reassuring words and kept his dreams at bay. Who was she? Where was she?

He needed to find her.

He rubbed his face, then swung his feet over the side of the bed and sat up. The room whirled before his eyes, and a wave of pain rolled through his head. He braced himself and waited for the room to still and the pain to subside.

Angels stared back at him. He swiped a hand over his eyes, then looked again. Porcelain angels in various poses and sizes sat on the shelf before him. They wore beatific smiles and cherubic expressions. And there were a lot of them. A veritable flock.

With a curse he surged to his feet. The room tilted wildly. "Dammit," he muttered, waiting for the world to right itself. He rarely waited for anything, and the idea that he was incapacitated made him feel as surly as a wounded bear.

His reflection in the dresser mirror caught his

attention. He was wearing only his briefs. She had taken off his clothes, and he wasn't sure he liked the idea. If there was any undressing to be done, he wanted to be the one to do it. Being stripped without his knowledge made him feel vulnerable, a feeling that was both foreign and abhorrent to him.

And he had never been more vulnerable or more exposed than he had been last night. Dammit!

He glanced back at the bed's blue sheets and fluffy comforter. The bedding was almost the color of her eyes, a clear, heavenly blue. Continuing his inspection of the room, he saw a straw hat circled by a band of flowers dangling from one of the bedposts, a white wicker bird cage planted with ivy and hanging from a hat rack, a pair of tennis shoes resting on the cushion of a blue plaid armchair, and a . . . harp.

A harp? Yes, there was a lap-size harp atop her dresser, the same kind of harp held in the arms of hovering angels, as he had seen in pictures. A whisper of air shivered over his skin, as if someone had opened a window and a breeze had blown in. Or as if a nearby angel had fluttered her wings.

Disturbed, he opened the closet door and found his black suit hanging alongside dresses, blouses, skirts, and pants, all smelling of that delicate, enticingly sensual, exceedingly feminine scent he had come to know as hers.

Frowning, he reached for his slacks, but his shirt was nowhere in sight. Then he saw a man's black turtleneck sweater. His scowl deepened. Was she involved with some man? His angel?

Muttering a curse, he grabbed the clothes and

went in search of a bathroom. A quarter of hour later he emerged, showered and dressed and ready to find her.

Haloed by the morning sun, she was sitting at the kitchen table, sipping a cup of coffee and reading a newspaper. He leaned against the door-jamb, partly because all his activity had left him light-headed, and partly because he felt the need to take several seconds to absorb the picture before him.

There were windows on two sides of the kitchen, most of them raised to let in the fresh, clean morning air that stirred the blossoms of the red and yellow potted flowers lining the windowsills. She was dressed in a pair of jeans and a white pullover sweater, and her hair was pulled back and tied in a ponytail by a long scarf, the ends of which trailed down her back.

And she still looked like an angel to him. An extremely desirable angel.

"Good morning," he said, his voice unexpectedly gruff.

Her head jerked up. "Good morning. I heard you in the shower, but I'm surprised to see you in here and dressed. I thought after the shower you'd go back to bed." She was braced to deflect any hurtful comment he might make about the easy way she had accepted his kisses last night, had, in fact, been practically liquefied by their heat.

When he didn't say anything, she relaxed. "Did you find the towels and toilet articles I laid out for you?"

He nodded, and immediately regretted the movement. "Thank you." Favoring his left leg, he limped to the table and dropped heavily into a seat across from her.

"Is your leg giving you a lot of trouble?"

"It's bruised pretty bad and a muscle or two may have been wrenched, but I don't think anything's broken."

"That's good," she said, relieved to hear Matthew's diagnosis affirmed. She poured him a glass of orange juice from the pitcher already on the table, then handed it to him. While he drank thirstily, she took the opportunity to study him in the full light of day. He had shaved the night's beard from his face, and what she saw held her practically spellbound. He wasn't handsome, but he conveyed an aura that was forceful, magnetic, and compelling. She was in more trouble than she had thought.

He held out the glass to her. "Could I have more, please?"

"Certainly," she said, refilling his glass and handing it back to him. His eyes were more the green of dark jade than black, as she had thought. But perhaps they darkened to black when he was in extreme pain. Or when he was in the throes of extreme passion. She quickly censored her thoughts. "I'm glad to see you up and moving. I've been very concerned about you."

He grimaced. "Last night I thought I'd died."

"I know. We talked about it. Remember? For awhile you thought you were in hell."

His eyes narrowed. "I remember."

She stiffened, waiting for a cutting comment, but it never came.

"I was sure I was in hell. There was just one thing that kept bothering me. *You.* You were an anomaly in the whole scheme of things. Angels aren't supposed to be in hell."

She had decided that being neutral and polite would be the appropriate way to act this morning, but he undermined her resolve. Her smile came readily. "No, I suppose not."

"There's a harp on your dresser."

"Yes, I know. I've played for years."

He considered her for a moment. "When I first saw you on the road yesterday, you had wings."

She burst out laughing. "I don't think so."

He set the glass of orange juice down and tilted his head to one side, absurdly wishing to reach across the table and bring her closer to him so he could explore and examine every inch of her and find out exactly who and what she was. Last night in the middle of his pain and fear, he had made a connection with her, and to say he was bothered by what had happened was an understatement. "You had wings yesterday."

He sounded so definite, she thought, still amused. "I'm sure I didn't." He continued to stare at her, his eyes hard, yet with the certain ability to stir her. "Are you hungry?" she asked, seeking a subject that would get his mind off his fixation of her as an angel.

"Yes."

"Great. How about—"

"But I don't want to eat yet. I want to know why I thought you had wings."

He was obviously a man who possessed a logical, analytical mind, she thought wryly, and he wasn't going to let this go until he understood. With a sigh she cast her mind back to the moment he would have seen her. "Let's see. I had just come up from the beach, and I was crossing the road—"

"What were you doing on the beach?"

She smiled to herself. He was determined to examine every aspect of what had happened. "Walking. I usually take a walk every afternoon."

"What were you wearing? I know it was white."

She nodded. "White jeans and a white sweater."

"Your hair wasn't pulled back like you have it today. It was loose and blowing with the breeze."

One pale brow lifted in mild surprise. "You saw a lot in those few seconds before you hit the brakes."

His strength might have failed him, he reflected grimly, but at least his instincts and training had held true. And he wanted an explanation for the beautiful, nearly luminous creature who was sitting across the table from him. "I saw an angel."

She chuckled, and his face hardened.

"You laugh easily."

"Yes, I do, I always have. But I'm sorry, I'm not laughing at you. I'm really not. I'm laughing at the situation."

"I don't think the situation is very damn funny at all. I'm in more pain that I've ever been in my life, I'm still not sure exactly where I am, and I look at you and see something that up to this point I've never believed existed. An angel. You."

She repressed an inexplicable urge to giggle. He was right, she thought. His situation wasn't funny, but after worrying about him all night, she was simply happy to see him up. "Okay, okay. Let's see—was I wearing anything else?" She snapped her fingers. "I've got it. I was wearing this scarf." She reached behind her and lifted one end of the white chiffon scarf that tied her hair. I had wrapped this once around my neck, and it's conceivable that the ends were blowing in the breeze behind me."

At last satisfied, he nodded. "Wings."

She refused to allow herself to laugh, but her eyes held a pronounced twinkle. "So, do you think you could eat an omelet now? Do you feel any nausea at all?"

"A little, but I may just be hungry." Annoyance creased his face. "I'm feeling shaky." He didn't want to add that his legs felt like rubber.

"That's natural after what you've been through."

"Maybe, but I think I probably need to try to eat something, and an omelet sounds good. If you wouldn't mind . . ."

"Not at all."

His eyes followed her every movement as she rose, went to the stove, and soon had eggs, cheese, and mushrooms cooking in a skillet. So she was a woman—an *angellike* woman—with kisses that made him forget everything and think only of her, and she had a way about her that could slip beneath his guard. He needed to be wary of her until he could leave. "Where's my car?"

Spatula in hand, she angled her body so that with a glance she could either monitor the cooking omelet or look at him. "We had it towed to Whit's."

"What's a Whit?"

"He's the only auto mechanic we have here in

Paradise, but he's good. Very good, in fact. He's a master mechanic who used to work in Los Angeles and Indianapolis. He came here to retire, but he's never quite gotten the hang of retirement. He still works every day. You can call him after you eat."

"I'll go see him," he said firmly.

Her first impulse was to tell him he needed to rest today, but she didn't feel inclined to challenge the determined glint in his eye. "If you like."

His gaze traveled around the cheerful multicolored kitchen. Dented but shining copper pots hung on a Peg-Board on one wall. Another wall held a white iron baker's rack that contained cookbooks. And more angels. He looked back at her. "Is your name really Angel?"

She smiled. "My full name is Angelina Smith. But I've been called Angel since I was a baby." She folded the omelet in half and lightly pressed down on it with the spatula.

"A blond, blue-eyed, ivory-and-cream baby," he murmured. "That's understandable."

He was giving her one of those looks again, she thought, feeling warmth creep up her neck. It was a hard, estimating look, as if he were trying to size her up and fit her into a category. She wondered why the simple classification of *woman* wasn't good enough for him. "What about you? You told me your name was Satan, but your driver's license says you're Nicholas Santini."

He gazed broodingly at the glass of orange juice in front of him. "Satan's a nickname that was given to me in the service, and it's stuck."

"How did you get the nickname?" As she had sat

beside him in the night, she had wondered and speculated about it.

"I guess people thought it fit." A muscle twitched along his jawline. "Only my parents still call me Nicholas."

"Okay," she said slowly, trying to gauge his moodiness. "Then you want me to call you Satan?"

"No."

Well, that was certainly clear enough. She slid the omelet, light as air, onto a plate, crossed to the table, and set it before him. "Coffee?"

He shook his head, causing pain to slice through his skull with sickening intensity. "Dammit."

"What's wrong?"

"Nothing." He closed his eyes, aware that he had practically snarled. But his accident, his injuries, and the angelic woman across from him all made him mad as hell. He wanted to be 100 percent well again, and he wanted to change her angelic look to one of wanton passion. He opened his eyes, and when the pain had subsided to a dull throb, he lifted his hand to touch the bandage at his left temple. "Did you do this?"

"No. Matthew did."

"Matthew?"

"Matthew Godwin. He's our local doctor."

"Let me guess. He's the only doctor in town."

His sarcastic tone made her defensive. "Yes, and we're lucky to have him. He's one of the best in the state. I'm sure he'll be by to check on you this morning."

He stared at her, wondering why he couldn't

seem to get enough of the sight of her. "Did you say *God*win?"

Instantly forgetting her pique, she smiled. "You're not going to start that again, are you?"

He might, he thought, if she kept smiling at him like that. "This Matthew has a deep, booming voice, doesn't he? I heard him last night, but I didn't see him."

She nodded. "He examined you before you came to, treated the gash on your temple, and stayed with you until he made the decision that you'd be all right."

"His voice was almost godlike."

She chuckled. "You don't give up, do you?"

"Very rarely."

"Well, let me tell you something. You may be in Paradise, and I may look like an angel to you, and Matthew may have a deep, booming voice, but you're alive, and on the planet Earth, and on your way to recovering from your accident. You're definitely not in heaven."

"Then why do I have the sensation that I am?"

He wasn't joking, she realized. He hadn't even smiled when he had asked the question. In fact, she realized she had yet to see him smile. "I don't know, Nicholas."

His eyes went to her lips. She had said his name so softly, so sweetly, and so unknowingly seductively. He wanted to see her lips form his name again, and then he wanted to kiss those lips. But most of all, he wanted the damned pain in his head to go away, because there was so much more that he wanted to do to her. This angel was capable of great passion. *His angel.*

"Why don't you try to eat something," she said gently. "Maybe it will make you feel better."

Something about her voice made him do as she bade. He definitely needed to find a defense against her.

He cut into the omelet and forked it into his mouth. "It's delicious," he said. "Thank you."

"You're welcome."

His gaze on her, he took a drink of the orange juice. "You stayed up all night and watched over me, didn't you?"

She shrugged, indicating what she had done was no big deal. "Most of the night. Starting around dawn, I slept for a few hours."

"You must be tired."

"Not really." It was the truth. There was an incredible amount of energy running through her veins, and she had the certain, unnerving feeling he was the cause.

"You've put yourself out quite a bit for a stranger."

"I was happy to do it." In fact, she couldn't have *not* done it. From the moment she had seen him pulled from the car, she had felt almost as if it were her mission to care for him. "The accident was partially my fault. I was out there in the middle of the road."

He didn't smile, but his lips twisted sardonically. "You're not guilty of a thing, believe me. I'm an accident waiting to happen."

"Don't you mean you *were* an accident waiting to happen? You spoke in the present tense."

"Did I? Well, it doesn't matter." He took another bite of the omelet.

She watched while he ate, thinking that she had been right about his not remembering the kisses. He had given no indication at all that he did, and she was relieved, she told herself. But at the same time she felt a perverse, nagging annoyance. How could something that had affected her so much leave him completely untouched?

Unable to finish the whole omelet, he pushed the plate away, then propped his elbows on the table and gazed at her. "I asked you to stay with me last night, didn't I?"

She supposed it was natural that he remember at least a part of what had happened. But that being the case, how could he have forgotten the kisses? "Yes. You said I helped keep the dreams you were having away. Do you remember the dreams?"

Remember? he thought increduously. The dreams had invaded his life, overtaken him, and now refused to leave. He accepted the torment as his due, but he couldn't, wouldn't, talk to her or anyone about them. And he hoped he hadn't revealed too much while he had slept. "Did you undress me?"

Coffee sloshed in the cup she was holding as her hand jerked. She set the cup down. "No. Matthew did." But she had seen his hard, muscle-contoured body, had in fact shamelessly drunk in the sight.

One dark eyebrow arched. "And did the good doctor also leave me this sweater?" He indicated the turtleneck he was wearing with a wave of his hand. "I found it in the closet, along with my slacks."

She nodded. "Matthew brought it over for you.

Your shirt is stained with blood. I have it soaking."

He had put off asking whose sweater it was until he couldn't any longer, and he was disquieted because ultimately he had given into the urge. And he still didn't know if she was involved with anyone. She could be having a relationship with the doctor for all he knew. Dammit. He didn't want to think about his beautiful, radiant, desirable angel kissing anyone else, much less having sex with that person. "I'm sorry," he said suddenly.

She looked at him blankly. "Excuse me?"

"I'm sorry about last night."

She stiffened. "Which part?"

"All of it. First of all, I'm sorry for putting you in danger by driving too fast. And then I'm sorry that you had to witness the crash. It must have been awful for you."

"I was terrified for you," she admitted, recalling how frightened and sickened she had been, watching the car spin out of control and then hearing the horrific sound of the crunching metal and breaking glass. In her shock she had screamed.

"I'm sorry for that. And I'm sorry for keeping you up all night." He paused. "And for disturbing you with my dreams." He paused again. "And for kissing you."

He *remembered.* And he was sorry. *Sorry?* Wonderful. Simply wonderful.

"You were there taking care of me, comforting me, and I took advantage of the situation. I'm sorry."

She pushed away from the table and marched over to the sink. It wasn't as if she wanted him to remember their kisses as having been rapturous and orgasmic, she told herself huffily. And since he had been an expert at stirring heat and desire in her, she was sure there was a legion of women he had given the same experience to. But it might have been nice if he'd acknowledged that their kisses had been at least *mildly* earth-shattering to him.

"Angel? Is there something wrong?"

"Of course not. What could be wrong?" She reached for the skillet and dropped it into the sink with a clang. She had to face it, she thought, utterly amazed at the confession she was about to make to herself. His apology had severely dented her pride. Well, heck. She gave the faucet a vicious twist and turned on the water.

He'd upset her, he thought, but he had felt that he should get what had happened between them out in the open. He could still remember the impact the kiss had had on him. As hellish as he had felt, he had almost caught fire. But she had to have been unnerved by a total stranger forcing a kiss on her as he had. It was a wonder she was even speaking to him. Still, she *had* seemed sunny and cheerful, until he had apologized to her. He pressed a hand to his head. Damn this headache of his. The pain was probably keeping him from thinking straight. "Look, I really am sorry—"

She whirled around, wet dishcloth gripped in her fist. "I heard you the first time. You don't have to say it again."

Three

"Good morning."

The deep, booming voice cut across the tension and drew Nicholas's attention away from Angel to the doorway. The man standing there looked like Abraham Lincoln dressed as a lumberjack. He was tall and thin, with a long, narrow face, gray-flecked black hair, and a matching beard. He wore a plaid flannel shirt and heavy-duty work pants, and he clutched a black bag in one hand.

The good doctor, Nicholas decided.

And, he was delighted to see, the doctor was about sixty. Too old, he instantly judged, to be involved with Angel. *His angel.* Dammit! He rubbed his head, wondering if he had suffered any brain damage in the accident. He simply had to quit thinking of her as his.

"I let myself in the front door and followed the smell of the coffee," the doctor said in a booming jovial voice. "I hope you have some left."

In spite of her lingering irritation with Nicholas over his apology, Angel grinned at her longtime friend. "Plenty."

He turned toward Nicholas. "Well, well, our patient survived the night. Those medical correspondence courses I took were worth it after all."

Angel's grin turned wry, and she looked at Nicholas. "That's Matthew's idea of a bedside manner. He only gets away with it because, generally speaking, his patients are a captive audience. Nicholas, meet Dr. Matthew Godwin. Matthew, meet Nicholas."

Matthew walked around to one end of the table, dropped onto a chair, plopped his medical bag down on the floor beside him, and fixed Nicholas with a keen gaze. "I bet your head feels like you stuck it in the Liberty Bell just as someone cracked it."

The doctor's words came out in a cannonlike volume that made Nicholas wince. "Would you mind speaking a little softer?"

Matthew gave a rueful grin. "Sorry. My voice gets away from me sometime, but it's great for calling hogs."

"You don't have any hogs," Angel said dryly.

"No, I don't. But I'm still a young man. I may get some. And if I do, I'll be ready." He switched his attention back to Nicholas. "So how are you feeling?"

"The Liberty Bell analogy sums it up pretty well."

"Mm-hmmm," Matthew said in the infuriatingly noncommittal tone common to his profession. He reached down beside him to open the bag.

Angel's sympathy got the better of her. "Naturally, you feel awful. Concussions aren't anyone's idea of a party."

"I have a concussion?"

"Definitely," Matthew said. "However, the good news is I think it's a relatively mild concussion—as concussions go, that is."

He rubbed his head. "You couldn't prove it by me."

"Mm-hmmm. Besides your head, what else is bothering you?"

"I'm limping, and my body feels as if I've been run over by about a dozen tractors."

"Plus a herd of elephants, I imagine," Matthew said cheerfully. "But that doesn't surprise me. By now I'm sure you've seen your bruises. Your whole left side probably looks like an elongated Rorschach test. The passenger side of the car took the impact."

"I'm sure it's easily repaired," Nicholas said testily. "I have to get back on the road today." He heard Angel make a sound behind him, but when he tried to turn his head, the doctor gripped his chin to keep him facing him.

"The only road I want you to travel today is the one back to bed, young man."

It had been a long time since anyone had called him young man, he thought irritably. And the doctor's countenance had stayed disgustingly jolly while he delivered the ultimatum. But then, Nicholas thought sourly, when a man had a voice like God, he wouldn't have to stoop to disapproving expressions to get his point across.

Angel moved around the table and sat down across from Nicholas, wondering at the soft sound of distress that had escaped from her when he had said he was going to leave. He was a traveler, coming from one place, going to another, with a whole life someplace else. Had she really thought he would stay? And did she really want him to?

"Okay," Matthew said to him, "now look straight ahead."

Nicholas did as Matthew asked while a small light was flashed into his eyes.

"Mm-hmmm."

His impatience got the better of him. "Look, just give me a clean bill of health and I'll be on my way."

Matthew threw back his head and laughed with glee. "On the off chance that I could give you a clean bill of health, which, by the way, I can't, just what do you think you're going to be on your way in? That red Ferrari of yours looks like a tin can ready for the recycling bin."

Maybe it had something to do with the way his head had again begun to pound, but Nicholas was appreciating the doctor's humor less and less.

"Any nausea?" Matthew asked.

"Some."

"What about dizziness and double vision?"

"Some dizziness," he admitted, then thoroughly fed up with not only feeling, but also being treated, like an invalid, he stood up. The room whirled before his eyes, and pain thundered through his skull. With a moan he sank back into the chair.

The doctor reached over and patted his arm. "Going to have to take it a little slow for a few days, son."

If there was one single thing he hated more than anything else in the world, Nicholas thought, it was going slow. But he just might have to give into the doctor on this one.

"Did you get any rest, Angel?" Matthew asked as he efficiently wrapped a blood-pressure cuff around Nicholas's arm and took his blood pressure.

"I got a few hours," she said, eyeing Nicholas's pronounced pallor with concern. She didn't have to perform any medical tests to tell that his pain had increased.

Satisfied with the reading on his instrument, Matthew unwrapped the cuff and stuffed it into his bag, then held out both his hands toward Nicholas. "Grip my hands as hard as you can."

Nicholas did, and was disgusted to realize his grip had lost its usual strength.

"Mm-hmmm." Matthew sat back. "Okay, well, I think it's safe to prescribe a painkiller for you."

"I don't take painkillers."

"If you're going to heal, you need to rest. And if you're going to get any rest, you're going to need some of that pain knocked down to a bearable level."

"I don't have time to rest."

"Mm-hmmm. Your schedule is very impressive, I'm sure. But you're not going to be any good to yourself if you don't take time to heal." He dug into his bag and took out a bottle of pills. He uncapped the bottle, and handed Nicholas one. "Take this."

Nicholas eyed the pill suspiciously. "What is it?"

"It's a mild painkiller. It'll take the edge off that thunder going on in your head."

"I told you, I don't take medication."

Matthew's gaze was kind. "I lose patients very

rarely, and then only when their time is up on this good earth of ours. Now I figure your time isn't up yet, because, son, yesterday you had one hell of an opportunity to buy the farm. But we pulled you out of that car of yours alive, and I'd take it real personal if you did anything to change that outcome. Take the pill."

Nicholas glanced from the pill to the doctor, then back to the pill again. "It's mild?"

"That's what I said, didn't I?" With a smile hovering around his mouth, the doctor watched while Nicholas reluctantly swallowed the pill with the help of some orange juice, then he lifted his bag into his lap and snapped it shut. "Angel, I'll write out a prescription for some more of those and have someone bring it over."

"That's fine."

"You better give the prescription to me now," Nicholas said, "because I'm about to call a taxi to take me over to this Whit's to get my car. I've got to get back on the road."

Matthew sighed and glanced at Angel. "I guess I should have checked his ears too. Besides being as stubborn as a mule, he apparently has a hearing problem." He looked back at Nicholas. "Call whoever it is that you're in such an all-fire hurry to get to and tell them you're going to be here for a few days."

Nicholas opened his mouth to object, but Matthew continued, rather like a tank, slow, steady, and unrelenting, Nicholas thought with ill humor.

"I went to school a lot of years to become as smart as I am. In fact, you have no way of knowing it, but my medical expertise is actually legendary.

People have been known to write songs about it, sonnets even. Really. You're going to have to trust me."

He didn't feel well, Nicholas thought suddenly. Exhaustion and pain were pulling at him. And the thought of climbing back into bed was an increasingly alluring one. "But I can't stay here."

"Is there a problem with his staying here, Angel?" Matthew asked, his eyes alight with a new interest.

"No, of course not." Matthew had known her since she was one day old. She had to be careful, or he'd suspect there was something wrong. And there wasn't. Not really. It was just that, at the present moment, her heart was thudding like a bass drum. She had a small house, with only one bedroom. If Nicholas stayed, the close confines were bound to present problems. Plus the memory of the kisses they had shared still hovered between them like some sensual specter, disturbing and tantalizing. Yet in spite of everything, she didn't want him to leave. Not right away.

The doctor looked from one to the other, then back at Angel. "Everything will be fine. I know I can trust you to look after my patient."

"If you can't trust an angel, who can you trust?" Nicholas muttered. He had the distinct impression the entire percussion section of a symphony orchestra had just taken up residence in his head and were performing with gusto.

The doctor's black brows rose with surprise, then his long, thin, weathered face crinkled into a wide grin, and he gave a laugh that to Nicholas's sensitive ears sounded more like a bellow.

"You're absolutely right. Well, good, the matter is settled then." Matthew stood up. "I'll check on you tomorrow, son. In the meantime, take it easy, and if you need me, give me a call. Angel knows the number." He gave another loud laugh. "Everyone in town knows my number."

When the doctor had left, Nicholas propped his elbow on the table, rested his pain-heavy head on his raised hand, and gazed across the table at her. "If I stay here, I'll be putting you out."

"Not that much," she said, adopting a neutral tone. A tingling and totally inappropriate tension had invaded her nervous system now that they were alone again. He affected her far too much. An attitude of distant politeness would help keep her unexpected guest at an emotional distance. *She hoped.* "Besides, you're not in any shape to go anyplace. Matthew said so, and I can see it for myself. You look like you're about ready to fall out of that chair, and your eyes are almost black."

"I have green eyes."

"Most of the time I'm sure you do. But they're black now, and they were black last night. You're not doing real well right now, Nicholas. Admit it."

He rubbed his hand over his face. "It's probably that damn pain pill. It's made me groggy."

Her grin appeared with alarming ease. Under the circumstances she couldn't help but find his stubbornness funny. He really had no choice but to give in to the inevitable and allow his body to recuperate. Yet because of his obviously strong nature, he was having a hard time yielding to what he perceived as a weakness. He would be a formidable man when he recovered. "Part of that may be the pill," she conceded, "but it's also your condition."

"You've done so much for me already. I don't want to impose."

He felt terrible, but he was still concerned about her. Her heart warmed. So much for emotional distance. "It's all right. Really."

"Are you sure? If you'd call me a cab, I could go to a motel or hotel."

She laughed. "There's no cab service in town. There's also no hotel. We do have a small motel, but it's being renovated. Very slowly, I might add."

Why was he trying so hard to get away from her? he wondered wearily. She was the most extraordinary being he had ever known. Her laughter was magically potent, and its golden resonance enslaved him every time he heard it. Light clung to her, making every other thing or place in the room seem dim. And she was offering to take care of him. Why was he arguing?

But there was one more question he had to ask. He lifted his head from his hand so he could look at her straight on and see her reaction. "Do you live here alone?"

"Yes."

He felt enormously relieved, and he told himself it was because he wouldn't be putting anyone else out by staying here. There were other things he wanted to ask her, questions that might go a little ways toward explaining her, but his ability to remain upright was about to give out. "If you don't mind, I think I'll go lie down for an hour or so."

"I'll help you," she said, quickly standing.

More slowly, he pushed himself back from the

table and got up. "That's not necessary. I can make it by myself."

"I'm sure you can," she said, coming around the table to his right side and draping one of his arms over her shoulder. "But you don't have to this time."

He wasn't used to anyone having to help him do anything, but he realized his pride was working overtime and without cause. If the truth were known, there had never been a time in his life when he needed help more. And he wasn't just thinking of his physical injuries.

She was partially supporting his weight while they walked into the bedroom. Her soft curves pressed into him, and the warmth of her body radiated right through his skin. She was a dream he must have had a long time ago, he thought. And now he had conjured her up, drawing her to him through the pain and torment of what he'd gone through during the past year.

"Here we are," she said, helping to ease his long frame down onto the bed.

He collapsed onto the bed with gratitude.

She watched him, her throat tight with emotion. Seeing him in a weakened state, pale, exhausted, and in pain, stirred her compassion. And something more that, for the moment, she was unwilling to think about. "Do you want to undress so that you'll be more comfortable?"

"No." Now that he was lying down, he was unsure if he could get back up again. "I'll be fine."

She stepped to the foot of the bed and took off his shoes. Then she raised the covers over him.

His hand shot out to grasp hers. "I don't know how, but I'll pay you back."

Every time he touched her, no matter his intent, she felt heat. She definitely needed to get a grip on herself. "Don't be silly," she said, patting his hand, trying to regain detachment. "I don't want any repayment. You saved my life."

"And you may be saving mine."

She smiled. "You only feel like you're going to die. In a few days you're going to be back to your old self." And then he would be gone.

She didn't understand about saving his life, he thought, his eyes drifting closed. He wasn't sure he did either.

"Can I get you anything before I leave?"

His eyes flew open again. "You're going to leave?"

"I'll just be in the next room."

"The next room?"

"The kitchen." She hesitated, hearing the tinge of panic in his voice. "Do you want me to stay with you?"

"No, no." He couldn't bring himself to ask her. "I'm only going to sleep for an hour." Surely, the dreams wouldn't come. It was daylight, and there was no question that he was better.

"Okay, then, but if you change your mind, just call out." She turned to leave.

"What will you be doing while I'm asleep?" It was a stupid thing to ask, he reflected, but for some reason he really wanted to know.

"I don't know. I guess I'll probably fix something."

"Fix something?"

"It's what I do. I fix things."

It made a kind of sense, he thought, keeping his eyes on her until she left the room. An angel would repair broken things. And he was broken.

It *did* make a kind of sense.

The last thing he saw before he fell asleep was the flock of angels hovering high above him, watching over him.

When he awakened, it was late afternoon, and a wonderful smell was coming from the kitchen. He took a moment to assess his condition. Rest had reduced his headache to a low, bearable throb, and the aching of his bruised body to a dull soreness. That was good. Using caution, he sat up. The room spun, but soon righted itself.

He visited the bathroom, grateful to discover his limp was less pronounced, then headed for the kitchen.

Angel was there, sitting cross-legged atop the kitchen table with a toaster in her lap, a screwdriver in her hand, and various parts scattered around her. A woman he didn't know stood at the stove, stirring something that was obviously responsible for the wonderful smell he had awakened to.

Angel looked up and saw him. "Oh, you're up. Great."

"I didn't intend to sleep so long. You should have awakened me."

"Sleeping is the best thing you can do for yourself," the woman at the stove said with a smile. She wiped her hands on the apron she was wearing, crossed the room to him, and held out her hand.

"Hi. I'm Jane. I'm a friend of Angel's." She was an older woman with calm gray eyes and her hair drawn back into a bun.

"I'm"—he hesitated—"Nicholas."

"Well, it's very nice to meet you, Nicholas." She pointed to a chair. "Why don't you sit down, and I'll get you something to drink."

"That sounds good, but first . . ." He looked back at Angel and felt his jaw tighten. She was so lovely. "Would you mind if I used your phone? I need to make a long-distance call, but I'll use a credit card."

"No problem. There's a phone in the living room." She waved her screwdriver, indicating the general direction.

"If you tell me what you'd like to drink," Jane said, "I'll have it ready for you when you get back. Soft drink? Iced tea? Milk?"

"Iced tea would be fine."

Jane nodded and waited until he had left the room, then turned to Angel with astonishment on her face. "Good grief, you didn't tell me the man was an authentic hunk."

Angel's lips twisted wryly. "A *hunk*, Jane? At your age?"

"Age hasn't left me blind, honey, and that man's a certifiable, dyed-in-the-wool hunk."

Angel bent her head over the toaster. "He's all right, I guess."

"If he was any more all right, I'd have to check myself into the hospital for treatment of heart palpitations. Where does he come from? Is he married? What does he do for a living?"

Married. She had discarded the possibility, but

now that she thought about it, the absence of a ring did not necessarily mean he was single. "I don't know any of those things," she said, trying to sound as unperturbed as possible, although a sudden, inexplicable depression had gripped her.

"Boy, are you slow."

"Give me a break, Jane. The man was unconscious."

"I know for a fact he was awake this morning. Matthew told me."

Angel sighed. "Maybe those things you asked are none of my business, or for that matter, yours either. Have you ever thought of that?"

Jane shook her head. "No. But never mind, just leave everything to me."

Angel laid down the screwdriver and fixed her with a level gaze. "I am not going to let you interrogate him, Jane. Nicholas has been badly hurt."

Jane serenely poured out the glass of iced tea she had promised. "Don't worry, honey, I'll be so gentle, he'll never know he was touched."

"Hi, Hawk. It's me."

"*Satan.* Lord, man, I was about ready to sound the alarm. You're about eighteen hours overdue."

Nicholas fingered the bandage at his temple with a grimace. "I know. I guess you could say I've been unavoidably detained."

"Did something happen?"

"Yeah. I've been in an accident."

"*Damn.* How bad? Are you all right?"

"The Ferrari spun out of control and hit

something—what, I'm not sure. I was knocked out cold. I woke up with a headache that hasn't gone away since, plus a mass of bruises, but other than that, I wasn't seriously hurt."

"Flying with the devil on your wings again, were you?"

Or an angel, he thought. "Something like that. And fortunately, no one else was hurt."

"That's good at least. Hey, didn't I tell you to catch the plane back with Blare and me?"

Ice slid down his spine, and his heartbeat accelerated. He *couldn't* fly, not ever again! His gaze darted wildly around until he saw a long shelf of angels directly across the room from him. A multitude. Their presence made him feel better. "My plan to drive home would have worked if it hadn't been for an unexpected curve in the road. As it is, I'm going to be a little late, that's all."

"How late?"

"I don't know yet, but not too late. Listen, until I get back, shut down Lightning One. Switch the people you can to our other projects, and give the rest a few days off."

He heard silence on the other end of the line. Then, "Are you scrapping Lightning One or simply postponing it?"

Damn good question, he thought. The project had been his obsession, but it had already cost him more than he could afford to lose in a lifetime. Was he willing to lose more? "I simply need some time to rethink it."

"All right." Hawk paused. "Where are you?"

"You wouldn't believe me if I told you," he said,

staring at the angels. "In fact, I'm not even exactly sure."

"That doesn't sound like you. Are you certain you're okay?"

One of the angels seemed to have taken flight and appeared to be hovering about an inch off the shelf. He rubbed his face and looked again. She was back on the shelf. "I'm fine." *Just having a nervous breakdown, that's all.*

"Look, why don't you put someone on the phone so I can get directions, and I'll come pick you up?"

"No."

"Why not? The passenger seat in my car folds down. I could make you comfortable."

"That's not necessary. I plan to check out my car tomorrow, and I'll probably head home pretty soon after that. Just expect me when you see me. Okay? And if there's a change of plans, I'll call."

"All right, if that's what you want."

"It is. See you soon."

Nicholas hung up the phone and wondered why he had turned down Hawk's offer. If he had given the word, he could be home by noon tomorrow. He pinched the bridge of his nose with his thumb and forefinger. Why had he turned Hawk down? There was no doubt in his mind that he could make the trip. Why?

He raised his head, and for the first time surveyed his surroundings. Angel's living room was small, but with a big window that looked out on a yard that sloped downward about eighty feet to a road that curved out of view. Between the two big trees that grew at the bottom of the yard, he could see a spectacular view of the ocean. That road must have been the one he had been on when he'd crashed, he decided.

He switched his gaze back to the room. It was furnished simply with a love seat and armchairs, all slipcovered in a cheerful print. Crocheted doilies lay in the center of the coffee table and the two end tables, and pretty knickknacks sat here and there. It was a comfortable, appealing room, but there were no family photographs on display anywhere. Nothing except the angels, all safely grounded at the moment.

Damn, there were a lot of them.

He pushed himself up from the chair and went in search of the real thing.

Four

"I think this stew is about ready to eat," he heard Jane say as he walked into the kitchen.

"And just in time," Angel said, giving him a big smile as he came through the door. "It's Jane's special chicken-stew recipe. She came over this afternoon to make it especially for you."

Her smile caught him unaware, hardening his body, softening his insides. Oh yes, he thought. The real thing.

"That's very nice of you, Jane." He sat down. "If it tastes anything like it smells, it's going to be delicious."

"It will be." Angel slid off the table, the reassembled toaster in her hand. "Your toaster's fixed, Jane."

The older woman didn't look up as she ladled the stew into three bowls. "Great."

Nicholas frowned at the various toaster parts left on the table. "Did these come from that toaster?"

"Yes."

"And it still works?"

"Yes."

"How?"

Angel shrugged.

Jane laughed. "We've all been asking that question for years, but nobody's come up with an answer yet. Angel has a way with broken things. She fixes what can't be repaired. It's sort of magical."

Angel had returned to the table with a sponge and was cleaning its surface.

"How do you do it?" he asked.

She looked at him. "I don't know. I just do it."

He told himself he wouldn't let the lack of explanation bother him. But it did anyway. "Did you go to a trade school?"

"No."

Jane set a glass of iced tea and a large bowl of stew in front of him. "No one taught her either. The thing is, she's always had the ability, almost from day one."

He didn't look comfortable, Angel decided as she brought three place settings to the table. "Would you like another pain pill, Nicholas? Jane got your prescription filled. Shall I get one for you?"

"No. I'm okay. And, Jane, remind me to reimburse you after dinner."

"That's fine," she said, unconcerned. "By the way, I also retrieved your suitcase from your car at Whit's and brought it. I figured you'd need you things."

"Thanks. I appreciate that." He waited until sh had taken a seat at the end and Angel had sa down across from him as she had this morning. "What did you mean when you said Angel had the ability almost from day one?"

Jane gave Angel a loving smile. "She came to me when she was one day old. I was head of the orphanage here in town, and I literally found her in a basket on the doorstep. My first look at her mended my broken heart."

Angel chuckled. "You're such a softy, I could have been a homeless puppy and you would have felt better." She turned to Nicholas to explain. "Her heart was broken because the number of kids at the orphanage had dwindled over the years, and those who were left were growing older."

"That's right," Jane said. "Plus the orphanage was running out of money, and I was afraid I was going to have to close it. But then Angel appeared, and I knew everything was going to be all right. And sure enough, old Mr. Smith, the town's local curmudgeon, died on the evening of the day she arrived and left his estate to the orphanage."

"That was lucky." It was also a little bit eerie, he decided, and didn't help one bit in explaining Angel to him, not in the concrete, substantive way he wanted.

Jane nodded. "I gave Angel his last name. I figured it was only right."

"And how did you decide on her first name?"

"Would anyone like to talk to me?" Angel asked.

Jane grinned at her. "In a minute, honey. You see, Nicholas, the basket I found her in was one of mine that I had inadvertently left sitting on the doorstep. She wasn't wrapped in a blanket, and she didn't have a stitch on. There was no evidence whatsoever that could tell me where she had come from, nothing to connect her with this earth. She simply appeared out of the blue. *Heaven.*"

Nicholas felt light-headed and drew his bowl of stew closer. Nourishment was bound to help. He ate several spoonfuls, then asked, "So the orphanage was able to continue?"

"For a while, but it's gone now. When the last older orphan left, I bought a house and moved Angel in with me. Now I own and run the local pub. When you get better, you'll have to come visit me."

"I probably won't be staying that long, but thank you for the invitation." He looked over at the luminous, blond-haired creature sitting across the table from him. An Angel would be hard to leave behind and even harder to forget. She would definitely remain with him in his mind.

"Were you able to make your phone call?" Jane asked him. At his nod she continued tranquilly, "I'm sure your family was happy to hear from you."

"Fortunately, my parents don't keep close tabs on my schedule. They're retired and living in Arizona." Even though Angel's head was bowed as she ate, he had the odd notion that she was listening.

"Then you're not married?"

All his senses were attuned to Angel, and he was aware when she tensed. "No." She resumed eating. He tore his gaze from her and saw that Jane's brows were arched expectantly. "The person I called was a longtime friend. We work together. I live in northern California."

Jane leaned toward him. "What do you do?"

"I'm an aeronautical engineer. I have my own

company, Santini Aeronautics. We design, develop, assemble, and test airplanes."

"How interesting. Isn't that interesting, Angel?"

Angel fixed her with a meaningful gaze. "Your stew is wonderful. You really should eat some."

"In a minute. Nicholas, do you fly the planes as well as design them?"

His spoon stopped halfway to his mouth. Slowly, he returned it to the bowl. "Not anymore."

"Then you used to. Why did you stop, and what kind of planes did you fly before you did?"

"The insurance company won't let me fly the planes I design, and I've flown several types." He hadn't told her all, and yet he was vaguely surprised that he had said as much as he had.

"That's smart." Jane paused to take a bite of the stew.

Angel attempted to curve the conversation toward something else. "I've never even been in a plane before."

Nicholas looked at her. "But then you wouldn't need to, would you? You're an angel."

Jane laughed merrily. "Poor girl. I'm surprised she hasn't gone to court to change her name legally. With her looks people are always making jokes about her being an angel. And I'm sure by now you've seen the angels that friends have given her over the years."

"They're hard to miss," he said dryly. "May I have some more stew?"

"Of course." Jane jumped up, and Angel turned the subject to the weather and then went on to engage Jane in a discussion about her sewing

projects and the sale going on at the local depart-
ment store.

As she'd hoped, Nicholas soon excused himself
and went back to the bedroom. Jane stayed to help
her clean up, then left.

And once again Angel found herself alone in the
house with Nicholas.

The floor lamp was on, and he was propped up
in bed, staring thoughtfully at the angels on the
shelf.

"How are you feeling?" he heard Angel ask from
the doorway.

"You have only one bedroom, don't you?"

Her mouth went dry. She nodded. "But don't
worry. I'll sleep on the couch."

"I'll take the couch."

Having already thought the situation through
beforehand, she shook her head. "Besides being
too short for you, the couch is too soft. You need
more support."

He leaned his head back against the headboard
and stared at her. "You could sleep in here. I
wouldn't bother you."

Her heart stopped, then started again with a
heavy thud. "I'll sleep on the couch."

He'd been lying, he thought. It would be impossible for him to lie next to her and not reach out
and pull her to him. He'd kiss her, but he wouldn't
stop there. He'd have to be dead not to make love to
her. And apparently he wasn't dead, only bruised
and concussed. He wanted her—more and more as
the hours went by.

"Would you like me to bring you a pain pill?" she asked, reaching for a normal tone and failing. To her ears, her voice had sounded amazingly husky.

"Maybe later."

"Okay, then, I think I'll get ready for bed. If you need anything, call me."

"How do you call an angel?" he asked softly.

"Angel," she said shakily. "Just say Angel."

She retreated to the bathroom and took a long, hot shower. Standing beneath the pulsating water, she reflected that her heightened senses really called for a cold shower. She had never in her life been so aware of a man. It was as if God had put an internal trigger in her that would activate sexual awareness the day she met Nicholas Santini. A part of her had actually wanted to say yes when he had said she could sleep in the bed with him. It was a part of her she didn't recognize and didn't know how to handle.

But he would be leaving soon, she reflected, and then her skin would no longer prickle, her heart would maintain a constant, even beat, her thoughts would no longer stray into tantalizing thoughts they had never been before. Her life would be normal. And strangely empty.

He heard her come out of the bathroom and pass the door. "Angel?"

"Yes?"

She came to stand in the doorway, and his breath got trapped in his throat. She was wearing an oversized white T-shirt that stopped midthigh, leaving long, shapely legs exposed to his view. How had he missed noticing how sexy her legs were? he wondered incredulously. He must have been concussed worse than he had thought. But then again, he hadn't missed her beautiful face or her lips that tasted like fiery bliss and looked as if they never lied. He had also noticed how sensually alluring her hair looked when it cascaded around her shoulders and down her back as it was doing now. And then there were those endlessly blue eyes of hers that reminded a man of heaven and beckoned him to her.

She might be an angel, but he wanted her as he would a woman. It was just another sin to add to his long list.

"Nicholas? Can I get you something?"

Calling out to her had been an impulse. He had wanted to see her one more time before he fell asleep, hear her voice, maybe even touch her. But he couldn't tell her that. And there *was* a question that had been bothering him. "How did I get here?"

She frowned. "You mean how did you get here in my house? When your car spun out of control, it went through my fence at the bottom of the yard, slowing you down some, and then you hit one of the trees. I ran up here and telephoned for help and—"

"No, no. I mean how did I happen to get on that road? I had been on the interstate, driving along the coast. But I wasn't on the interstate when I crashed. I was on a two-lane blacktop road."

"Several miles back, the interstate curves inland for about ten miles. At that point there's a turn that puts you onto our road." She gestured toward the front of her house. "But the turn is well marked. I don't know how you could have gotten confused. You must not have been concentrating."

With a sigh he rubbed a hand over his face. "I was driving home from my best friend's funeral. I don't think I'd slept since he was killed."

She gasped and took several steps toward him. "Nicholas, I'm so sorry."

"So am I."

His sadness touched her heart and drew her a few steps closer. "How was he killed?"

"The plane he was flying crashed."

"Did he have a family?"

"Parents. They live in Washington State. That's where the funeral was."

She edged nearer until her thighs touched the bed. He could smell her scent, he could almost feel the heat of her body. Was he talking to her because he wanted her to stay with him? Or because he needed to talk to someone, anyone, and who better than an angel? He didn't know. His intentions were mixed up in his mind. He grasped her wrist and pulled her down onto the bed beside her.

Drawn to him, she went with no resistance. She had known his soul was tormented, and now she knew part of the reason. "What was his name?"

He had never been able to share his pain easily, but for some mysterious reason it felt right to tell her. "Jazz. I'd known him ever since flight school."

"Was Jazz his nickname or his real name?"

"It was his nickname and his call sign. Most pilots have them. In Jazz's case, he earned his because he loved jazz. He'd listen to it in the cockpit even though it was against the rules, and

I can't tell you how many concerts he dragged me to."

"Was Satan your call sign?"

"Yes."

"And how did you earn it?" For the first time she saw him smile, except it was a smile of irony, not humor.

"Everyone said I flew with the devil on my wings, so they called me Satan."

He still held her wrist, but she couldn't bring herself to point it out to him. "What does that mean, flying with the devil on your wings?"

"It means I had no nerves back then. I could pull off any maneuver, no matter how tricky or reckless, and get out of any situation, no matter how dangerous. I had the devil's luck with me."

"I'm sure skill had a lot to do with that luck."

He stared at her. "I think someone somewhere must have really screwed up when they allowed someone as innocent and good as you to come into my life."

She laughed unsteadily. "I think you've got that wrong. You came into my life."

"I guess I did, didn't I?"

She laughed again. "Yes, and as a matter of fact, you broke the speed limit getting into it."

"Maybe I knew what I was doing after all." His eyes darkened. "You smell like every fresh, sweet female thing I've ever smelled." His hand slid up from her wrist, and he wrapped his fingers around her upper arm. "Come here."

"I—I need to leave so you can rest."

"Angels give aid and service to the sick and the

suffering, don't they? Well, I'm both. Give aid and service to me, Angel."

"I'm not an angel."

"I'm beginning to believe you're *my* angel."

She pressed her free hand against his chest. "Nicholas—"

"I know," he muttered. "I already know all the reasons why I shouldn't do this. But I'm going to have to do it anyway." He curved his other hand around her neck and pulled her down until his lips crushed hers.

He couldn't account for how much he needed this kiss, he thought hazily. It was a need that was crawling through him, tightening his gut, hardening his muscles, firing his blood. He plunged his tongue deep into her mouth and heard her moan softly. A man could find ecstasy with her. Paradise.

But even as he thought it, he knew it couldn't be. Paradise wasn't for him. There was too much guilt, bitterness, grief, and anger in him. He had his own hell to live in, and it wouldn't be fair to take her with him. Surely, though, he could kiss her for just a little longer. . . .

He was teaching her yet another new lesson about kissing, she thought. She hadn't known a kiss could be addictive and soul-destroyingly hot. She should never have allowed this. She should have been firm. She shouldn't have wanted it so badly.

The strength with which he held her told her that his condition had improved. Soon he would leave. And she would lie in this bed, alone at night, and remember the man who had made her feel both earthly doubts and unearthly pleasure.

His hands smoothed down her back to her hips,

and he grasped her bottom, moving her against him until she could feel the physical evidence of what the kiss was doing to him against her lower body. A fire started to spread slowly through her.

He shouldn't be doing this, he thought. Why didn't he stop?

She shouldn't be doing this, she thought. Why didn't she stop?

He wouldn't be good for her, he thought. She wouldn't be good for him. "Angel—"

He was grief-stricken, she thought. Under normal circumstances he wouldn't be doing this. He wouldn't even be here. "Nicholas—"

He let his hands drop away from her.

She pushed away from him until she was sitting up. Her hand trembled as she lifted it to brush her hair from her face. "Whatever you do, don't say you're sorry."

It was an easy request for him to agree to, because he wasn't sorry. "All right."

"In the morning we will have both forgotten this."

If she could forget the kiss they had just exchanged, she was a better person than he was. "I'm sure you're right."

"Good, then that's settled." She chanced a glance at him and saw that his eyes were onyx black. Passion, she thought with a silent moan, not pain.

He hoped it was settled. He had always been determined to avoid situations such as this, where reason and logic might not rule. In the past he had shunned serious involvement because of the potential danger it might bring. And even now, when his occupation had changed, his instincts were telling him to walk away. But . . .

"Good night." Without waiting for him to say anything else, she rose and left the room.

Moments later, lying on the couch, she reflected on what had happened. She had wanted to end the kiss, and apparently so had he. And she was glad. She was convinced that it had been the right decision for both of them. But if that was truly the case, why did she feel this incredible letdown? She certainly wasn't ready to consent to go to bed with him. And even when that time came, then what?

In an amazingly short period she had come to care for him. She could tell herself twenty-four hours a day that the reason was rooted entirely in her unalterable tendency to repair broken things. She could tell herself that, but she wouldn't believe it.

Rain was falling gently the next morning as Angel drove him to check on his car, and Nicholas was gratified that their conversation was easy and without tension. He had decided to try to make what little time they had left together as pleasant as possible, and he speculated she had made a similar decision.

He had had a restless night, but hadn't dreamed or called for her, a major achievement. And that morning he seemed to be thinking more clearly, though a vague ache lingered in his body, more because of her, he guessed, than because of the accident.

He gazed out of the car's window, liking what he

saw. Paradise had a rustic flavor to it, and an overwhelming sense of peace. Even though it was a small town, they had already passed a couple of churches, a supermarket, a school, and even a library. The one- and two-story buildings were built out of logs or sided with shingles that had weathered over the years until they looked as if they'd come off old boats. The houses had character and personality, and the yards were green, with beds full of blooming flowers.

The town appealed to him in a deep, basic way. Lately his life had been like a pressure cooker, full of stress and tension, and this place was almost like a tranquilizer to him.

Angel wasn't going over the posted speed limit, but for once in his life he didn't mind the slow pace. It was such a simple thing to do, sitting as a passenger, letting someone else drive him. *His angel.* He was content. He even had the maverick wish he could stay a little longer.

"You know," he said, "by rights this car of yours shouldn't run. I've never seen a car quite like it. You didn't even use a key to start it. You just sort of touched something. And it almost looks as if you've taken about four or five different cars—none of them, I might add, made before 1969—and put them together."

She sent him a grin. "That's pretty much what we've done over the years."

"We?"

"Whit and me. When I turned sixteen, he found me an old junker of a car. We kept changing it, updating, and adding on, until we got to this present version."

"And what about that cherub hood ornament?"

"That was Whit's idea. He found it somewhere."

"Well, I have to concede the car runs great. I wish I had the time, I'd love to study it and see what you've done."

She fell silent, wondering why she had the absurd desire for their time together to go on a little longer. She would only hurt more when he left.

She turned the car into a gravel driveway and pulled up in front of a big barnlike building. He climbed out, grateful that though his left leg still throbbed, the limp had diminished until it was barely perceptible. Angel came around the car, carrying an umbrella, and held it over his head as they walked. It had been a long time since anyone had taken care of him as she was doing, he reflected. Strangely, he was responding to her and her care as if he were a dry sponge, soaking it all up and wanting more.

Inside the building Nicholas caught the unmistakable scent of oil and grease. Cars in various stages of repair sat here and there. Classical music wafted softly through the air. Then he saw Whit. He was standing beside a Thunderbird, wiping his hands on a rag.

Angel waved at Whit and took Nicholas's arm to guide him forward. "Come on, I'll introduce you."

Whit's uniform was a pair of well-worn, grease-stained overalls. He wore a pleasant expression and had gray hair that went everywhere but into a neat hairstyle.

Whit held out his hand. "Been wondering when you'd make it in. Wasn't holding my breath, though. The doc said you were pretty banged up."

Nicholas nodded cordially. "I'm better now. How's my car?"

"Wish I could say the same for it. Must have been a beauty before the wreck. It's a shame, but now it's totaled."

Nicholas felt a hint of his old tension creep back. "If you can't fix it enough for me to be able to drive it back home, I can get a tow truck here and take it there. I know I can find someone there who can do the job."

Instead of being offended, Whit chuckled. "Hold on there, young man. Given time and the parts, I can fix anything that has wheels on it. I've worked on both race cars and street cars, foreign and domestic, and I have the setup here to do the job. But one look at your car by an insurance adjuster and he's going to total it. And there's something else you should know—"

"Forget the insurance adjuster. *I'll* pay."

Angel touched his arm, drawing his gaze. "Why are you being so insistent about repairing this one? Why don't you go ahead and get a new one?"

Pain flared in his eyes. "Jazz gave the car to me last year. There was no special occasion, he did it just for the hell of it. He saw it and thought I should have it. It's the last thing he ever gave me." He turned back to Whit. "Where is it?"

Whit gestured toward a corner. "There."

Nicholas turned and froze. The left side of the car was totally caved in, the frame bent, the door torn away, the steering wheel askew, the windshield shattered. From the looks of it he should have been killed. For most of his adult life he had flown over twice the speed of sound and never crashed once. Hell, he hadn't even got a scratch. But then on a back road in Oregon, going less than a hundred miles an hour, he had nearly lost his life. It was more than ironic, it was damned odd.

Angel touched his arm. "Are you all right?"

He pressed a hand to his head. "I think so."

"I'd say it was a miracle you're here today," Whit said. "Yes, sir, a downright miracle. Someone upstairs must have sure been looking out for you."

His angel. "Can you repair it, or would you rather I call a tow truck?"

Whit shrugged. "I can do it if you're willing to pay. 'Course, it's going to take a little time to get all the parts I need from the Ferrari people. And there's one more thing—"

Nicholas pulled out his billfold, retrieved a credit card, and handed it to him. "Order the parts and have them expressed to you."

Whit glanced down at the credit card. "Sure thing. Can I reach you at Angel's?"

She saw Nicholas hesitate. No matter what her previous thoughts on the matter had been, excitement at the prospect that he might stay a while longer sent her pulse rate out of control. "You're welcome to stay. In fact, I'm sure Matthew would say you should. I know you're feeling better, but you're still not a hundred percent yet."

"We'll talk about it." He took her hand and began walking for the door. "I'll let you know where I'll be, Whit."

"Wait up there. There's something I need to tell you."

Nicholas glanced back at him. "What's that?"

"Your car's brake line—it was sabotaged."

Five

Angel spun around. *"What?"*

Nicholas's movements were slower as he turned back to Whit. "I beg your pardon?"

"Your brake line was sabotaged."

For some reason he couldn't seem to take in what Whit was saying. "Don't you mean the brake line cracked or was punctured when I crashed?"

"No, sir, I don't. What was done to the line may be the reason you crashed, though."

Nicholas waved his hand in the direction of his wrecked car. "Look at the damage. Whatever it is that you found had to have been done when I crashed."

Whit gazed unblinkingly at him. "I've never known an accident that could shave a brake line."

He felt so stupid, as if he had to have everything repeated, and even then it didn't make sense. "It looks as if it's been shaved?"

"Methodically and meticulously."

"No." He could hear his own heartbeat, and he was aware that something was very wrong. He just wasn't certain what it was. "You've got to be mistaken."

"But I'm not," Whit said calmly. "I've been working on cars too many years to mistake a thing like that. Sometime, somewhere, someone shaved the brake line, and when you slammed on the brakes, the sucker blew."

"Angel's hand had turned cold in his, he noticed. And even more alarming, he no longer seemed to have the ability to drive air in and out of his lungs. Plus his heartbeat was loud, *too* loud. Through the years he'd always paid close attention to his mechanics, and now his instinct and training wouldn't allow him to discount entirely what Whit was saying. "I want to see for myself."

"I figured you would. Be my guest. Check behind the right front wheel."

His sore body demanded that he move carefully as he lowered himself to the concrete floor and positioned himself beneath the car. Once there, he had to consciously force himself to study the area involved because his mind was fighting against Whit's verdict. It took a couple of minutes before he could make himself accept what he was seeing.

"Nicholas, are you all right?" Angel called anxiously.

"Yes." *No*, he thought. He felt sick to his stomach. The brake line had blown, almost obliterating any sign of the tampering. Almost, but not quite. Someone had been very clever, but the evidence was there. With a curse he eased himself back out and stood.

Angel came up to him and put her hand on his arm. "What did you find?"

"Whit's right."

"Oh, no!"

Her eyes were such a clear blue, he had no trouble seeing the fear there. He reached out and squeezed her hand. "There's nothing for you to worry about."

"I'm not worried about myself, Nicholas. It's *you.*"

Even here, in this dim barn of a garage, she was lighted by a radiance that seemed to come from within. And she was worried about him. Wrenching his gaze away from her, he turned to Whit. "Who else have you told?"

"No one. I figured it was your business, and you could contact the sheriff yourself."

"Good. Thank you for being discreet."

Whit guffawed. "That's the first time anyone's called me discreet. No, I just figured you didn't need anybody poking around into your business until you were feeling better. I knew you'd be safe at Angel's."

As before, he felt a whisper of air shiver over his skin, as if an angel had just fluttered her wings. He glanced at Angel. As far as he could tell, she hadn't moved. He looked back at Whit. "How did you know I'd be safe there?"

Whit shrugged. "Just stood to reason that you would."

Nicholas rubbed his head, willing away the vague ache that persisted. He had to think. "Whatever your reason, I appreciate it. I'll contact the authorities later."

Alarmed, Angel reached out and gripped his arm. "If someone is trying to kill you, you have to do something now."

He put his hand over hers. "We'll talk about it when we get home."

"Home?"

Why had he said *home*? he wondered with sudden irritation. "I meant your house. Whit, save the brake line, and I'll get back with you."

"That's fine. In the meantime I'll get right on that car of yours, and let me tell you, it will be a pleasure. I haven't worked on that fine a piece of machinery since I left Indianapolis."

Angel's mind raced during the drive to her house. Violence was foreign to her; intentionally hurting another living thing was totally incomprehensible to her. But someone was trying to kill Nicholas, and it made her want to scream with outrage. How could he be so calm?

"Nicholas—"

"Not now, Angel."

Her hands tightened on the steering wheel. "Your head is so hard, I'm surprised it didn't protect you from a concussion."

He smiled tiredly. "Lately I haven't been protected from anything." Not even upset angels.

Once at the house, she busied herself in the kitchen. It wasn't long before Nicholas came in and sat down at the table. Without his having to request it, she poured him a glass of iced tea and one for herself.

"I hope you don't play poker," Nicholas said dryly,

"because you're pretty awful at concealing your feelings. If you had your wings on, your feathers would be standing on end right now."

She dropped into a chair and crossed her arms beneath her breasts. "This isn't funny, Nicholas."

"I couldn't agree more."

"Then why are you waiting to call the sheriff? You're in danger."

"Not at the moment. Whatever reason Whit had for saying I was safe here, he was right. It just so happens no one knows where I am."

"But yesterday you said you called a longtime friend."

"I did. Hawk. But I didn't tell him where I was."

"Was that deliberate on your part?"

"Not at all. Hawk is my friend."

"Well, somebody isn't. Nicholas, what are you going to do?"

He rubbed his head again, and his fingers brushed against the gauze bandage, bringing a frown to his face. "I don't know. I wish I did." Which wasn't like him at all, he reflected grimly. Plans and goals had always been a part of his life. But when he'd taken that wrong turn, his life had altered dramatically in more ways than one. He felt more vulnerable than he had ever felt in his life. Maybe his vulnerability stemmed from the fact that he hadn't gotten over the shock of Jazz's recent death, not to mention Rocky's death eight months ago. Maybe it was because his body was still recovering from the accident. Or maybe, simply, it was because of her blue eyes.

"This is nothing for you to be concerned about,

Angel. I promise, whatever happens, no danger will come near you. I'm leaving this afternoon."

Abruptly, she straightened. "You're going to do no such thing! You said it yourself. You're safe here." Her pale hair swished from side to side as she shook her head. "No, no. You're staying, and that's final."

In spite of all the reasons he had to cry, he burst out laughing. "I've flown over most of this world, and I've never found anyone like you."

Because she had never seen him even give a genuine smile, the impact of his laughter was twice as forceful. His laugh was rich and husky and skimmed along her nerves like a reading of a beautiful, erotic poem. "You were probably going too fast to notice."

"I think a more likely answer is that there are very few angels on this earth. You're obviously part of a rare and maybe even endangered species."

She had wondered what he would be like when he was better. Now she knew. Without effort he could mesmerize. She blinked. "You're evading the subject."

"The subject being?"

"You staying here. You need to, and I want you to."

He smiled, and she found it a perilously attractive smile.

"You'll never know how inviting and nearly downright impossible to refuse your invitation is, but—"

"But you're going to."

"Yes, I am. I need to get back home—"

"You called this place home earlier."

"That was a mistake." He felt the same irritation now as he had then. Didn't she know he could never have a permanent home with anyone, but most especially not with an angel? "Apparently, someone is trying to kill me, and I've got to figure out who it is."

"And you're going to go back home and do it?"

"Yes."

"That's like diving into a pool full of fish, knowing one of them is a shark, but uncertain which one it is. That's stupid, Nicholas."

"You don't understand."

"I understand completely. You have to decide who had the motive and opportunity, and you can do that here, where you'll be safe."

"No, Angel."

Her expression turned incredulous. "I'm surprised at your attitude. Were you ever a fighter pilot?"

"What?"

"Just tell me. Were you a fighter pilot in some branch of the service?"

"Yes."

"Then your pilot training should have taught you that you need to stack the odds in your favor before you fly into a dangerous situation. And you don't go if you're under par. You need to be at your sharpest, Nicholas, and right now you're not."

"The thing is, Angel, I don't want to put you in the way of my danger."

"How is that going to happen? You said yourself no one knows where you are."

As much as he wanted to argue with her, he couldn't. She was right—about his physical condition and about staying here. He would have a much better chance of surviving if he could remain inaccessible until he had figured out where the danger was coming from. He looked back at her and saw a luminous being, all ivory and cream, pale hair, and devastating eyes. *She* was a danger in herself.

He could rent, buy, or borrow a car and drive on down the road until he found a motel to hole up in. But how he wanted to stay. With her. He didn't know why, but somehow he felt she held the key to his healing. "This is a small house. I'll be in your way."

"We'll manage."

"I wouldn't want you to wait on me like you've been doing."

"All right, then I won't."

"I would want to pay for the groceries."

"Fine. Anything else?"

"Yeah, there's the sleeping arrangement. I should take the couch."

"We'll work it out." She paused. "Then it's settled?"

With a sigh he rubbed his head. "I guess so."

"Good. Now you need to rest. Why don't you go lie down for a while?"

He had nearly killed her, and he had presented her with nothing but problems ever since. And she still looked happy. How extraordinary. "Yes, I think I will." He stood and was nearly at the door when an impulse he didn't understand made him glance back at her. "Where will you be?"

"I'll either be here in the house or out back in the garage. That's where my workshop is."

"You don't plan to go anywhere?"

"No."

Satisfied, he headed for the bedroom, not to rest, but to try to think. He settled on the bed under the watchful gaze of the angels.

Someone was trying to kill him. At first he'd been stunned by the idea. Now, he felt absolute and utter astonishment. Why would anyone want to kill him?

He had no answers, and because he didn't, his gut was tightly knotted and ice had filled his veins. He was used to danger. His chosen career of fighter pilot and then test pilot had carried with it an inherent danger, but it was a danger he had a measure of control over because of his experience and skill. If a bandit approached, he could pick him up on his radar screen. If his plane malfunctioned, he had a chance of either landing it or ejecting.

But the danger that threatened him now had no face and no reason, and for the moment, all his experience and skill were worthless.

He heard Angel moving about in the kitchen and felt a contentment that, under the circumstances, was definitely strange. A couple of days ago, for a part of a second, he had contemplated driving straight into the sun and into blessed oblivion. Then Angel had stepped into his path. She had sheltered him and cared for him and given him strength with her presence until he could regain his own strength. She was still doing it.

He slowly closed his eyes, reflecting on the curious fact that, although he had never been in more danger, in many ways he had never felt safer.

• • •

When he awakened, he was surprised to see that he had slept for almost two hours. He lay still, listening for Angel, but the house was quiet. The rain had even stopped. Where was she?

Alarmed, he jerked upright and immediately regretted the action. The headache that had been with him since the accident was definitely going away, but unfortunately he still wasn't ready for sudden moves of any kind. With a colorful curse at his infirmity, he eased himself off the bed.

"Angel."

There was no answer. It didn't take him long to search the house and find out that she wasn't there. It was in the living room that his alarm turned to panic. What if something had happened to her?

He glanced at the angels. "Where is she?"

The garage. She had said she had a workshop in the garage. Of course. He threw a suspicious look at the angels, then went to quickly freshen up. Minutes later he was crossing the yard.

Angel felt a soaring sensation in her chest as she looked through the side windows and saw him approach. She had been miserable the last couple of hours, here, in the place where she was usually the most content. But her ability to repair things had deserted her, and the broken oscillating fan that sat on the worktable was a testament to her failure.

Nicholas had obliterated everything else from her mind. Whether it was right or whether it was wrong, she had come to feel a certain amount of possessiveness toward him. It had started that first night wen she had sat by his bed and heard the anguish that was tearing him apart. The feeling had been overwhelming today when she had found out someone was trying to end his life. It mustn't, it couldn't, happen. No matter what, Nicholas had to live.

She hurried to the door to greet him. "Hi. Did you have a good nap?"

"Apparently. I didn't expect to sleep at all, but I fell asleep almost immediately."

He was looking much healthier, she noted, more vital, and, heaven help her, more compelling. "I'm glad you were able to get some rest. Come on in." She held open the screen door, and he stepped in.

He gazed around the two-car garage. "This is your workshop?"

"Yes." She followed his gaze, trying to see what was making him frown, but everything looked normal to her.

A worktable took up the entire length of one wall. Above the worktable, hundreds of tools were grouped and hung on a Peg-Board. Appliances, clocks, televisions, fans, and other assorted things were arrayed either on the worktable or in shelves at the back wall. On the opposite side of the room, two big, old-fashioned, overstuffed chairs and a couch were grouped in a conversational arrangement with several tables and lamps. Three dogs of dubious pedigree lay around a potbellied stove that stood nearby. The entire area was carpeted.

"This is the neatest, homiest workshop I've ever seen."

She laughed and was somewhat startled by the sound. While she'd been waiting for him to wake up, her nerves had stretched until she had been sure they would snap. "I don't make much of a mess when I fix things."

"What do you do about the parts that are left over after you're finished?"

"I save them in various bins in the back. I never know when they might come in handy."

"Have they ever?"

She smiled. "Not yet. Make yourself comfortable, and I'll pour us some lemonade."

Still feeling the warmth of her smile, even after she walked away, he sat down on the couch. She went to an old refrigerator he hadn't seen, pulled out a pitcher, and then retrieved two glasses from a nearby cabinet.

When she handed him his lemonade, he stared at it with bemusement. "I can't remember the last time I had lemonade. I was probably just a kid."

She laughed again. "Well, are you going to drink it or just look at it?"

"Oh, I'm definitely going to drink it." She dropped down onto the other end of the couch, and he downed a portion of the cool liquid. "It's good."

"Thanks. I usually make a fresh pitcher every morning and bring it out here. It's refreshing and keeps me going."

He stared at her. "I would have thought you were more the type to make divinity."

"That's my favorite candy. How did you know?"

"Just a guess. Who are your friends over there?" He gestured toward the dogs. One of them raised its head, wagged its tail, then dropped its head back to the rug.

Angel smiled. "Larry, Moe, and Curly."

"After the famous Larry, Moe, and Curly?"

"That's right, and believe me, their names fit them perfectly."

"Why?" he asked, staring at the listless dogs.

Just then, one of them rolled over in his sleep and whacked the second dog with a big paw. The second dog opened one eye, apparently decided to get out of the way of the first, and rolled over on top of the third dog. The third dog woke up and snapped at the first one.

She laughed. "See?"

"I guess their names fit after all."

"They're strays that have found their way to me, and now they're part of my family."

"I haven't seen them before."

"They're usually running around the yard, but when it rains, they stay in here."

"I gather their place is by the stove."

She grinned. "They love that stove, even when there's no fire in it. Everyone should have a place they call their own, don't you think?"

"And your house and workshop are yours?"

She spread out her hands. "This is it. What's your place like?"

He shrugged. "It's a condo. Actually, it's a very *nice* condo, but I never seem to spent a lot of time there. I'm usually at work."

"And who's there?" she asked softly, taking the opening. "Who's at your work or at your condo who's trying to kill you?"

His expression darkened. "I don't know."

"You must know, Nicholas. How could you not?"

"I'm completely baffled." He took a few more swallows of the lemonade, then set the glass on a table. "You would think that, if a person hated me so much they wanted me dead, their hate would be so powerful I couldn't help but feel it."

Unconsciously, she shifted closer and angled her body toward him. "Even if you haven't felt it, you have at least one enemy, and you have to figure out who. Think for a minute. Could it be someone in your personal life, or maybe someone in your professional life?"

"It can't be personal, and as for professional, I can't think of a single reason that would give anyone a motive."

"Okay, then, tell me what you do know. Talk it out. Tell me what exactly it is that you do. Tell me who your friends and acquaintances are, your business associates. Tell me—"

"No. That wouldn't be a very good idea. You shouldn't be involved."

She reached out and touched his hand. "I can help, Nicholas. I want to."

Her delicate, feminine scent reassured him. She was unlike anyone he had ever known. She made him want her. She made him feel peaceful and safe. He knew he could trust her. He had already shared a portion of his torment with her. Still . . . "It's not that simple."

"Why not?"

"I don't know, Angel, I guess because nothing ever is."

He was obviously a self-contained man, and she had no right to push him to share personal details of his life with her. On the other hand, she couldn't sit idly by and not try to help him. "You said you were an aeronautical engineer and that you have your own business. And you also said you didn't fly planes anymore."

"I said the insurance company wouldn't let me fly the planes I designed. But every chance I got, I used to fly other planes."

"Why are you talking in the past tense?"

"Because that part of my life is over now."

"Why?"

He grimaced at her persistence, but it never occurred to him not to explain. "I've already told you that I was a fighter pilot. But what I didn't tell you was that I was in the air force, and it was one of the greatest times in my life. Our squadron was the best, bar none."

"Our?"

"Jazz was there with me. So were Hawk and two other good friends of mine, Rocky and Blare. We were all really close, and in the air no one could touch us. We were the best of the best. The five of us switched to being test pilots together, and we all got out of the service about the same time."

"Is that when you started your own business?"

"Yes. For years I had been obsessed with an idea for a new plane." He chuckled, but his tone remained flat and matter-of-fact. "One night in a bar I wrote the initial plans down for it on the back of a napkin. I called it Lightning One."

"Really? Tell me about it."

He shrugged. "It's a new type of jet fighter."

"Does the military need one?"

"There's too much at stake for the military ever to rest on its laurels. My jet is designed for greater speed, maneuverability, and accuracy with target, plus it has more durable parts and therefore a shorter downtime for maintenance."

"You must be very smart."

"I don't feel smart at all, not anymore. I was born with flying in my blood, and it was my dream to design and make this new plane. Those four guys I mentioned believed in me and came with me. I gave them all stock in the company, and we set out to develop my idea, and of course, along the way we took on other projects as well." His eyes clouded. "Now I'd give my life if I could go back and change their minds about coming with me."

"Why?"

"Because Rocky and Jazz are dead now, and Hawk was crippled in a stupid, unnecessary accident that to this day doesn't make sense. Actually, he was damn near killed, and when he did recover, he was left with a bad limp." He grimaced. "We were all so lucky when we were in the service, but in the last couple of years, our luck has really turned for the worse. I guess you could say we're being grounded one by one. Only Blare is still flying."

"What do you mean only Blare? There's you."

"No. I can't go up again."

He had cried out those same words in his sleep that first night, she remembered, and now she realized his eyes were once again nearly black. This time the cause was pain. "Why can't you?"

He fell silent. A minute stretched to another

minute. And when he finally spoke, his voice was low, broken, and rough. "I've lost my nerve. Hell of an irony, don't you think? The guy who always flew with the devil on his wings, the guy who was one of the best of the best, has lost his nerve."

"What happened?"

"Does something have to have happened?"

"I think so. You said yourself that flying has always been in your blood. Someone else didn't ground you. You grounded yourself, and it's killing you inside."

"How do you know that?" he asked in an odd tone.

"Isn't it?"

He closed his eyes. "Yes," he said, "but there's nothing I can do about it. I saw Rocky's Lightning One plane come down in flames, a plane I had designed, a plane that had been built under my supervision. He managed to eject, but he was seconds too late. He was on fire and unconscious by the time he hit the ground. We rushed him to the hospital, but there was nothing I could do for him except sit by his bed, day in and day out, watch him suffer, and die a piece at a time."

"I'm so sorry, Nicholas."

Slowly, he opened his eyes. "Don't be sorry for me. Be sorry for his wife and two-year-old son. Rocky was so proud of that boy." He shook his head. "Fighter pilots and test pilots have no business having a family."

"What?" she asked, surprised.

"You have to be alone in the cockpit," he said looking at her but talking almost to himself "When that life-or-death moment comes, you can't even for a split second, be thinking about a wife or kids. You have to be absolutely focused or . . ."

He trailed off, and she had the strangest feeling he had just erected a wall between them.

During that long first night he had said, "I'm sorry. It's my fault," and she had wondered what it was that he blamed himself for. "Do you think that's what happened to Rocky?"

He expelled a long, ragged breath. "No, not for a minute. My design caused his death."

"How can you be so sure?"

"There was an investigation, of course. They said their findings were inconclusive, but that it was more than likely pilot error. I didn't believe the report. No one who knew Rocky did. He was just too damned good. When we built the next plane, I checked, rechecked, and triple-checked everything until I was satisfied that it was safe. Then Jazz volunteered to take it up." He paused, remembering. "He was so excited and happy. We all were. Then the damned, bloody plane blew up right over the airfield, right above my head."

He stopped and studied the compassionate expression on her lovely face. He had already told her more than he had imagined he could, but somehow he knew that she wouldn't judge him, wouldn't blame him. Then again, she didn't have to. He was doing a good-enough job of it all by himself. "My confidence blew up with Jazz. I killed two of the best friends I ever had, Angel, and I can never go up again. Even the idea makes me break out in a cold sweat, and I'll probably scrap the Lightning One project as soon as I get back."

She reached out and put her hand in his, a simple, comforting gesture. "Who will that decision affect?"

"Me mostly. I'll be canceling my dream, but it has cost me too much."

He wasn't referring to money. "How will your company weather the decision?"

"It'll be all right. We have other contracts. I won't have to lay anyone off." He put two fingers to the gauze pad at his temple. "Angel, I don't want to talk about this anymore."

She squeezed his hand. "I know it's painful, but you have to. We have to figure out who would want you dead."

He had always met life head-on and had never backed away from anything. But he also never buried two friends in the space of a year and then been informed someone was trying to kill him. "Let's talk about you instead, at least for a little while."

"Just tell me this much. Is there anyone who would benefit from you closing down Lightning One?"

"No, but there'd be a lot of people who it would hurt. For one, the pilots who won't get to fly it."

"Who else?"

"The people who are working on the project have become dedicated to it, and it's going to hurt them to stop. Okay, now I've answered your question, answer one for me. Tell me why just looking at you soothes me."

She hadn't been prepared for the abrupt change of his mood. "I—I don't know."

"Then maybe you can tell me why looking at you also makes me want you."

He said it as if it were a known fact. And in truth she had known it. She released his hand. "You're not yourself, Nicholas. You've suffered one bad trauma after the other."

"You're right. I'm not myself. What else could explain my attraction to an angel?"

Agitated by his honesty, she twisted her fingers together. "Stop it, Nicholas. You know perfectly well I'm not an angel."

"Maybe I'd rather think of you as an angel. Mortals don't make love to angels."

"Nicholas—"

"Don't look so worried," he said softly. "I may want you like hell, but I can't have you. The fact that someone's trying to kill me makes remaining unattached more important than ever."

She glanced away, feeling unaccountably unhappy. What was wrong with her? She should be glad he felt as he did. "Most men wouldn't view having sex with someone they'd just met as becoming attached. In this day and age your attitude must be very rare."

With a finger against her cheek he turned her head so that she was looking at him. "No, you don't understand. *You're* the one who's rare. And I have a really bad feeling that if I ever got you in bed, once wouldn't be enough."

Heat radiated out from where he touched, gliding beneath her skin, over nerves, and into her blood. She wanted him, too, she realized.

He leaned toward her and lightly touched her lips with his. At the faint contact heat ignited, and the kiss went from light to hard in a microsecond.

She didn't resist. How could she? It would be folly to deny her response when her arms were already wrapped around his neck and she was edging closer to him. . . .

Six

"Angel, are you in there?"

At the sound of Matthew's deep, booming voice on the other side of the screen door, Angel jerked away from Nicholas and swiped a hand across her mouth, then immediately thought how stupid that was. A laser probably couldn't cut away the imprint of his lips; she could feel it in her soul. "Yes, come on in." She rose and hurried across the room to her workbench, putting space between herself and the two men until she could regain her composure.

The dogs managed to lift their heads and thump their tails against the carpet to show their pleasure that the doctor was there. Then they went back to sleep, all scrunched together, looking like a big wad of fur, feet, and tails.

Nicholas found the heightened color on Angel's face and neck far more interesting than he found the doctor, but he felt compelled to be civil. "How are you, Doctor?"

Matthew's bushy eyebrows rose. "You can certainly tell you're a stranger in these parts. No one ever asks me how I am. Of course, that's because they know I have the constitution of a locomotive and never break down." Matthew burst out laughing at himself. "Probably a locomotive on one of those bullet trains they have in Europe. Sleek, fast, and sexy, that's me. Right, Angel?"

"Right, Matthew."

"Did you hear that? She didn't even laugh." Matthew stepped closer to Nicholas, his demeanor confiding. "I'm so glad you crashed in our town. Everyone here has already heard my jokes."

He must be feeling better, Nicholas thought, because the man wasn't bothering him as much as he had. He glanced at Angel, but instead of meeting his eyes, she slid onto a stool.

"So how are you, young man?"

"According to Angel. I have a hard head."

The doctor laughed again. "Giving out medical diagnoses these days, sweetheart?"

"That one wasn't difficult," she mumbled, staring at the broken fan.

Matthew dropped down on the couch and deposited his medical bag beside him. "Well, son, I have to agree with her there. If we were going by the current shape of that automobile of yours, you should be stone-dead. It's a miracle, that's what it is."

What could he say? He had thought the same thing when he had first seen the car.

Matthew continued. "Unfortunately, in my business I don't get to see too many miracles."

"With Angel living here, I'm surprised you don't have more."

Matthew's eyebrows moved up and down. "Excuse me? On, I see, *angel*. That's funny. You're a funny young man. I hope you can stick around a while, or at least manage to crash here again some time in the near future."

"That's a lovely sentiment, Matthew," Angel said.

"Thank you, darling."

"Look," Nicholas said, "you don't have to examine me, I'm much better."

"Really? How interesting. I don't remember you telling me you were a doctor."

"I'm not, but—"

"Now that's a crying shame. Paradise has been a one-doctor town for as long as I can remember, and I could use some help, not that I'm getting old or anything. Right, Angel?"

"Right."

He snapped open his bag. "By the way, have you fixed that fan of mine yet?"

"What fan?"

"The fan you can't seem to keep your eyes off of."

Angel straightened with a frown. "Oh."

"Well?"

"I can't fix it."

Matthew looked at her. "I've never heard you say that before. Is something wrong?"

"No, of course not," she said irritably. "But, Matthew, the fan is ancient. You need to turn loose some of that money of yours and buy a new one."

"You don't seem yourself today, honey." Real

concern had taken all the levity out of Matthew's voice. "Are you running a fever?"

"Have you ever known me to run a fever?"

"No, but there's always the first time." Matthew's long legs propelled him up and across the room. In a matter of seconds he was pressing the back of his hand against her forehead. "You do feel a little warm. Now why do you suppose that is?" Matthew stepped back and eyed her with interest, as if she had suddenly come down with a disease he had never encountered before.

Her irritability grew. "Your hand isn't working accurately today. I don't feel warm, and what's more, I never felt better in my life." She threw an embarrassed glance at Nicholas and saw that his eyes were narrowed on her as if he were trying to figure something out. *Her*, no doubt. Being visually X-rayed by a man with Nicholas's force and magnetism was an experience she found decidedly unnerving. "Leave me alone, Matthew, and go back to your real patient."

"I will as soon as you tell me why, if you feel so darned good, your fix-it system is all screwed up."

She made a sound of exasperation and slid off the stool. "It's not, and I'm fine. Leave the blasted fan, and I'll repair it."

"But you said you couldn't fix it."

"I'll just have to work on it a little longer, that's all." She started toward the door. "For now, though, I'm going back to the house, and you and Nicholas can have some privacy."

Nicholas spoke up. "You don't have to leave on my account."

"Yeah," Matthew said. "You were there when I examined him before. What's up?"

She groaned. "It's simple, Matthew. Your examinations are boring." She walked out and banged the screen door behind her.

Matthew grinned at Nicholas. "Fascinating girl, isn't she?"

"Very. Did you say she has never run a fever?"

"Never. Even when she was a baby, she was never sick a day. She managed to skip all the usual childhood diseases. I remember one year when chicken pox was running rampant through the schools. . . ."

"Angel didn't catch it?"

"Nope."

"Don't you think that's a little strange?"

"Son, in my business, we use the word *blessed*."

After Matthew had examined him and left, Nicholas returned to the house. In the kitchen he found a pot of soup on the stove, along with a mug and a covered plate of sandwiches. Angel was nowhere in sight, but this time he managed to keep himself from panicking. As he had walked back to the house, he had seen her car. She had to be close by.

The phone on the kitchen wall caught his attention. He had told Hawk that if there was a change of plans, he would call, but a new inner wariness made him hesitate. Angel's questions had made him realize at least one thing. Whatever the reason his faceless enemy had for trying to kill him, it wasn't professional. It couldn't be. Lightning One would benefit too many people, and he had always been scrupulously fair with the government, his private contractors, and his employees. That left the personal side of his life. But that theory didn't make any sense either.

He stared at the phone. Dammit, he was acting like a fool! He owed it to Hawk and Blare to check in and let them know his plans. He jerked the phone off the hook and punched in the numbers. Blare answered the phone.

"Hi, it's me," Nicholas said.

"Well, hi there, stranger. Heard you got yourself banged up a bit."

"Yeah, something like that. Listen, there's a guy here who says he can repair my car, and I want to stay a few more days to make sure he knows what he's doing."

"That car's your baby. I'm surprised you're even letting some local yahoo touch it."

"He seems like a good man, and it will be less complicated all the way around if it can be repaired here."

"Yeah, I guess. Hey, listen, Hawk told me we're suspending work on Lightning One."

"I have to rethink some things, Blare."

"I understand your doubts, Satan, but I have to tell you, I think it would be a major mistake to scrap the project."

"Even after all that's happened?"

Blare was silent for a moment. Then he said, "Man, that plane's gonna make history one day. If only—"

"Exactly. If only. But I don't know what the hell is

wrong with it, and, Blare, you're the next one in line to take it up."

"Yeah, I know. Hey, forget the car. Come on back today. Let's figure out what's wrong and get on with it."

Rubbing his forehead, Nicholas stared at the angels on the baker's rack. Beautiful, winged creatures, they all wore wise, sweet expressions, and they seemed to be looking at him expectantly. He closed his eyes. *What in the hell was he supposed to do?* "Not just yet," he finally replied. "I need some time."

"At least tell me where you are and give me a number where you can be reached. If something happens, Hawk and I need to be able to get in touch with you."

"I'll check in with you, and don't worry, I'm not going to stay long." Glancing out one window, he saw the dogs romping in the yard, tossing and chasing an old tennis ball, running into one another and barking loudly.

"Jazz's death has hit us all hard, Satan, but you shouldn't put yourself out of reach. I don't like it. You've never done anything like this before."

"I know I haven't, but indulge me on this."

"Dammit, Satan, what's wrong with you? Why in the hell won't you tell me where you are?"

Nicholas expelled a long, heavy breath. What *was* wrong with him? He, Blare, and Hawk had been through too much together for him to treat them like this. "I'm sorry. I'm in Paradise, a little town on the coast of Oregon, and I'm staying with a very nice woman who helped me after I crashed. Her name is Angel Smith."

"Are those her dogs I hear?"

"Yeah." He heard an expectant silence from the other end of the line and knew what was coming next.

"You want to give me the number there?"

He didn't. He wasn't ready to be at the beck and call of the real world just yet. "It won't be necessary. I won't be much longer."

"Okay, then. Take care of yourself and keep in touch."

"I will. Good-bye."

He hung up the phone. Blare and Hawk didn't understand what he was doing, staying away from his work, remaining inaccessible to his friends. And he wasn't completely sure of his reasons either.

Except it was easy to be here. And it felt right. And almost essential.

He moved to the stove and helped himself to the food, ladling soup into the mug and selecting several of the sandwiches for his plate. Then, carrying the plate and mug, he went in search of Angel and found her on the front porch, sitting in a cushioned glider.

"Mind if I join you?"

Her hair fell away from her face as she looked up at him. "Have a seat. I see you found lunch, late though it may be."

He chose a chair next to the glider and propped his plate on his knee. "It looks delicious, but I don't like you going to so much trouble for me. A can of tuna fish would have been fine."

"I didn't have a can of tuna fish," she said dryly

"I happen to dislike tuna fish, but I'll be glad to go buy a few cans for you."

Her eyes were shadowed, making them a darker, more mysterious blue. "What's the matter?"

She shrugged and lied. "Nothing." She couldn't tell him how disturbed she'd been by her reaction to what had happened between them right before Matthew had shown up. But then, ever since he had arrived, she had been experiencing strange, unfamiliar feelings that had no rhyme, reason, or explanation.

"Is there someplace we can go out and eat tonight so that you won't have to cook?"

"Sure. We can go to the pub. Jane would be delighted to see you again."

"Good, let's do that then." He took several sips of the soup.

"What did Matthew say?" She leaned forward and eyed his left temple. "I see he changed your bandage."

"According to the good doctor, the stitches have to stay a while longer." He grimaced. "I didn't even know I had stitches."

"I'm not surprised. You've had a lot of other things to think about."

She was right, though probably in a different way than she had meant. His preoccupation with her had grown, until she was in his mind night and day, cluttering his thought processes, scrambling his logic and judgment. And in some puzzling way she even took precedence over his trying to figure out who wanted him dead. "Tell me something."

There was a softness in his tone that put her on guard. "What?"

"Why is it that I haven't seen any sign of a boyfriend or boyfriends?"

She cleared her throat. "Just because you haven't seen one doesn't mean—"

"I've been here long enough that if someone was pursuing you, he would have called or come over by now."

She sighed, put out with herself because she felt as though he had caught her in some dastardly deed. "It's no big deal, Nicholas. I've done my share of dating, but I long ago decided that I'm kind of like my dogs—"

He smiled. "I would never in a million years make that connection."

"But it's true. I happen to be one of those strays in the world who's never meant to link up with that one special person."

"Your dogs found you."

"Okay, maybe the dogs were a bad analogy."

"They definitely were." He paused. "In all these years you never found out who your parents were?"

"No." She stared toward the distant ocean. "You heard Jane. There was nothing that could link me to anyone."

"Except heaven. I remember."

She sighed. "The truth is not heavenly or even close to splendid, Nicholas. I was an abandoned baby. For whatever reason, someone thought it best to leave me on the orphanage doorstep. So I became one of Jane's orphans. More than that, I was the last of the orphans in Paradise." A pensive note entered her voice. "I've always thought there was a certain sadness about being the last of the orphans."

"Maybe, but you could also look at the situation another way. Since your arrival there've been no more orphans in Paradise. That's good. Besides, you don't strike me as the least bit sad. You laugh too easily."

"That's because for the most part I am happy. Jane and Matthew, plus a few other close friends in town, are my family." She shrugged. "It's just that sometimes I can't help but long for a . . ." She trailed off, aware that it wouldn't be wise to put her longing into words.

"What?"

Instead of answering him, she shrugged again. She loved Jane and Matthew with everything that was in her and had a unique relationship with each, but Jane was a mother hen to a host of other orphans, and Matthew belonged to the whole town. And in the secret regions of her heart she had always had a vague longing to belong to one very special person and have that person belong to her. Absurdly, the feeling had intensified a hundredfold since she had met Nicholas. But it was a problem she would have to deal with alone. "Don't get me wrong. I don't mope about my being an orphan. I'm realistic. And if I don't have a past, I've created a very nice present for myself."

He stared at her for a long moment. "You know what I think?"

"No, what?"

"I think the reason there are no suitors knocking at your door is because capturing an angel has proved too hard a task for the men around here."

Angel took hold of Nicholas's hand to lead him through the maze of people, as she followed Jane to one of the tall mahogany booths at the back of the pub. All around them, friends waved and called out hello. She waved back, but didn't stop to talk. She was sure the last thing Nicholas wanted was to be introduced to a pub full of people. But, she reflected wryly, coming here tonight had definitely been a good idea. The two of them had been alone with each other too much, and having people around them would help her put Nicholas and the way he made her feel into perspective.

"Is everyone in town here tonight?" Nicholas asked Jane as he and Angel reached the booth.

Jane's gray eyes twinkled with amusement. "No, it just seems that way. Does the noise bother your head?"

"No, I'm fine. I'm surprised, that's all. I didn't think there would be such a crowd here."

Angel slid to the middle of the booth's padded seat and gestured for him to take the other side. "The pub's nearly always full. Jane has a way of making everyone feel welcome."

Jane gave a dismissive wave of her hand. "Shoot, that part's easy. Coming up with menus that will have something for everyone takes some doing." She handed them each a menu. "Johnny will be over in a few minutes to get your order, and I'll be back later to see how things are going. Have fun."

Angel smiled at Nicholas after Jane had left. "She's a nice lady, isn't she?"

Her smile once again took him off guard. And it was the same smile she always gave him, the one that was unknowingly seductive, the one that had the power to make his muscles harden and his mind forget everything it should remember. He answered her question with a nod, while he took in how she looked.

She was wearing a blue cotton dress, with a low, round neckline, short sleeves, and a full skirt. He had never seen a simpler dress. He had also never seen a sexier dress, and he knew that it was she who was giving the dress the sex appeal.

She could feel the force of his attention on her skin like a white-hot spotlight, and the heat was almost overpowering. "So what do you think you'd like to eat?" she asked in an effort to diffuse the charged atmosphere between them. What ever had possessed her to think that a crowd would make any difference in their awareness of each other?

"I'm not sure," he said, his gaze steady on her. "What do you recommend?"

"Everything's good. Why don't you check out the menu?" *Because if you continue looking at me the way you are now, I'm going to melt.*

For a moment she didn't think he was going to, but he finally bent his head to study the menu, and she gave a silent sigh of relief. "Oh, look, Matthew has just arrived."

"I hope he doesn't come over here," he muttered.

She blinked with surprise. "Don't you like him?"

"He's a good man, but his jokes are pretty terrible."

She laughed. "He knows it, too, but he has a great time anyway."

Even in the midst of the noisy pub, her laughter sounded crystal and golden, like an angelic carillon. Wondering how he was ever going to be able to stay under her roof without taking her to bed, he set aside the menu. Now that he was stronger, his need for her was growing with each passing second.

Her skin had heated so that she didn't even have to look at him to know that his gaze had returned to her. "Uh, Matthew's going to another booth. He probably feels like we have already had our chance to laugh at his jokes today. What have you decided you want?"

He had decided what he wanted the minute he had opened his eyes and seen her. "I'm just going to have a steak and salad."

She nodded, giving the menu a final check, then closed it and put it down. "I think I'll have the same."

Actually, right at that moment, she felt incapable of making a decision on her own. Coming to the pub together had increased rather than alleviated the intimacy she had been trying to avoid. And sitting across the booth from him, doing something as mundane as discussing what they were going to order, was giving her a real sense that they were man and woman, not patient and nurse.

Several of the younger women were staring admiringly at him, and she didn't blame them. He was wearing a pair of navy slacks teamed with a blue sport shirt and a lightweight navy sport jacket. A gold watch gleamed on his wrist against the fine dark hairs on his arm. He looked heart-throbbingly masculine.

Their waiter, a teenager with a shock of blond hair and intelligent brown eyes, came bopping up to their booth. "Hi, Angel. How's it going?"

He had asked her the question, but his entire attention was focused on Nicholas. She smiled, understanding his fascination. "Great. How about you, Johnny?"

"Super. You know I'm coming up on my senior year."

"I did know that, and congratulations. I'm very proud of you."

He grinned, wiped his palm down his jeans, and extended his hand to Nicholas. "Hi, I'm Johnny."

"I'm . . . Nicholas." Funny, he thought. He had been called Satan for most of his adult life. But here it seemed right to be known by his given name.

"Nice to meet you, Nicholas, and I've got to tell you—you've got one awesome car. It's not enough that it's a Ferrari, but it's a *red* Ferrari." His expression knowing and serious, Johnny nodded his head. "That's the ultimate. I really envy you." At Nicholas's puzzled expression he explained, "I drop by Whit's on a regular basis. He knows just about everything there is to know about how machines and things work. I'm interested in becoming an engineer." He threw a grin at Angel. "And thanks to Angel, I just may make it. But anyway, even busted up like it is, that car of yours is flat-out beautiful."

"Thanks, Johnny. Maybe you and I can take a ride after Whit's through with it."

"That would be totally awesome!"

Jane passed by. "Take their order, Johnny."

"Oh, yeah, sorry." His grin turned sheepish. "What can I get you tonight?"

"We're both going to have steak and salad," Nicholas said. "I want mine rare. Angel?"

"Medium."

"Okay, I'll get that for you as soon as possible."

Nicholas eyed her curiously. "What was that reference about thanks to you he just might become an engineer?"

"Nothing, really."

"It didn't sound like nothing."

"Well, there was a time when he was having family problems, and he was thinking of dropping out of school. I talked him into staying in, that's all."

"That's all? Sounds like a lot to me."

She shifted in her seat, then tried to cross her legs, but she accidentally brushed a leg against his. The contact sent an electrical charge through her. "Sorry," she mumbled, embarrassed, but then she noticed he appeared oblivious to what had happened.

His gaze was thoughtful. "So you fix people too."

At that moment she didn't even feel capable of adding two and two. "Don't put too much emphasis on what happened with Johnny. He simply needed someone to talk to."

"And you were there, just like you were there for me."

His voice was husky and low and flowed over her.

tangling her senses and increasing her nervousness. Because she was afraid her voice would betray how he was affecting her, she shook her head, letting the gesture show that she thought he was wrong.

He glanced around the room and saw a man standing beside a booth, demonstrating his bowling technique. "Have you ever been out of this town, Angel?"

"Of course. When I was younger, Jane took me on several vacations. I've seen a lot of the United States."

"And I've seen all of the world. We're such opposites."

Something about the statement struck her as a challenge. "Are you talking to me or to yourself?"

"What if I was talking to you?" he asked thoughtfully. "What would you say?"

"I'd ask you what point you were trying to make."

"I'm not sure."

"Well, if your point is that, in general, opposites are not compatible, I've always found the exact opposite to be true. When two people are different, they each bring an element of the unexpected to a relationship, so things never get dull."

"Are you speaking from personal experience?"

She shifted beneath his sharp gaze, and with no other thought than that she suddenly felt warm, she attempted to cross her legs once more. Again, she brushed against his legs. Again, she felt heated electricity. "No, uh, personal observation." Lord, what was she trying to do? Talk him into a relationship or out of one? She had better make up her mind fast.

"You said you had dated. Did you date much?"

"Enough."

He stared at her. "You've never had a lover, have you?"

Color flushed her cheeks. "That's a very personal question."

"Yeah, you're right, it is. But you haven't, have you?" When she didn't answer, he sat back and stared at her. If the circumstances were different, if she weren't the kind of girl who could cause chaos in a man's life . . .

He would be the first. The idea twisted and turned through his mind, bringing him to the feverish point where he thought he was going to have to get up and walk out the door—away from her, away from temptation—before he did something he would regret.

"Why are we talking about me, anyway?" she asked. "You're the one with the problem, and it is monumental and deadly serious. We should be trying to decide what's the best course of action for you."

"We, Angel?"

She clasped her hands on the table in front of her and looked down at them. "You know what I mean."

"I've told you before. I don't want you involved."

"But you need help."

"No, Angel, I don't."

Behind them a tray of glasses fell to the floor with a loud crash, and reflexively he recoiled. Apparently, he was more tense than he had thought, he reflected ruefully. But the crashing sound served as a reminder of all the reasons why it wouldn't work out between him and Angel. What if the noise had been a gunshot instead of a tray of glasses? He had been too caught up with her to react quickly, and he wouldn't have been able to protect either of them.

Johnny returned with their steaks and salad, and Nicholas fell silent while he ate.

He had felt the same heated response she had when her legs had brushed against his; he was simply better at keeping his emotions under control. Long years of being a pilot had seen to that. No one was cooler under fire than he.

But Angel represented a new kind of fire, a new kind of enemy. Now more than ever, he couldn't become involved, not with her, not with anyone. He couldn't subject her to danger. And he couldn't subject himself to the danger of an involvement with her.

Involvement would soften the edges on his instincts, blunt his wit.

He had to remain cool.

Seven

"Is it hot in here to you?" Nicholas asked, frowning, when they returned home.

Outside, it was pleasantly cool, but the house did seem stuffy to her. "I'll open a few windows."

"No, I'll do it." He badly needed the activity. His whole body felt tight, and he had the peculiar sensation that his blood was rushing at an unnatural speed through his veins. If he thought he could manage it, he would go down to the beach for a run. But he felt strangely unsteady.

Annoyed and unsure why, Angel watched him as he flung open several windows. All evening, she had been having trouble with her nerves, and now they seemed more active than ever. Even the sound of his voice disturbed them, making the nerves prickle and pulsate. "I'll get the bedding for the sofa." She started for the hallway door.

"I'm sleeping on the couch tonight."

Passion awaits you...
Step into the magical world of

Loveswept

E N J O Y . . .

A Magical World of Enchantment Awaits You When You're Loveswept!

Your heart will be swept away with Loveswept Romances when you meet exciting heroes you'll fall in love with...beautiful heroines you'll identify with. Share the laughter, tears and the passion of unforgettable couples as love works its magic spell. These romances will lift you into the exciting world of love, charm and enchantment!

You'll enjoy award-winning authors such as Iris Johansen, Sandra Brown, Kay Hooper and others who top the best-seller lists. Each offers a kaleidoscope of adventure and passion that will enthrall, excite and exhilarate you with the magic of being Loveswep

- ♥ **We'd like to send you 6 new novels to enjoy—<u>risk free!</u>**
- ♥ **There's no obligation to buy.**
- ♥ **6 exciting romances—plus your <u>free gift</u>—brought right to your door!**
- ♥ **Convenient money-saving, time-saving home delivery!**

Join the Loveswept at-home reader service and we'll send you 6 new romances about once a month— <u>before they appear in the bookstore!</u> You always get 15 days to preview them before you decide. Keep only those you want. Each book is yours for only $2.25* That's a total savings of $3.00 off the retail price for each 6 book shipment.

*plus shipping & handling and sales tax in NY and Canada

Enjoy 6 Romances–Risk Free! Plus...
An Exclusive Romance Novel Free!

Detach and mail card today!

Loveswept

**AFFIX RISK FREE
BOOK STAMP
HERE.**

Yes! *Please send my 6 Loveswept novels RISK FREE along with
the exclusive romance novel "Larger
Than Life" as my free gift to keep.*

RD123   412 28

N A M E

A D D R E S S   A P T .

C I T Y

S T A T E   Z I P

MY ''NO RISK''

Guarantee

I understand when I accept your offer for Loveswept Romances I'll
receive the 6 newest Loveswept novels right at home about once a
month (before they're in bookstores!). I'll have 15 days to look them
over. If I don't like the books, I'll simply return them and owe nothing.
You even pay the return postage. Otherwise, I'll pay just $2.25 per
book (plus shipping & handling & sales tax in NY and Canada). I *save*
$3.00 off the retail price of the 6 books! I understand there's no obli-
gation to buy and I can cancel anytime. No matter what, the gift is
mine to keep–*free!*

SEND NO MONEY NOW.
Prices subject to change. Orders subject to approval. Prices shown are U.S. prices.

ENJOY . . .

♥ 6 Romance Novels–Risk Free! ♥ Exclusive Novel Free!
♥ Money Saving Home Delivery!

FREE BOOK OFFER
RUSH!

POSTAGE WILL BE PAID BY ADDRESSEE

BUSINESS REPLY MAIL
FIRST CLASS MAIL   PERMIT NO. 2456   HICKSVILLE, NY

LOVESWEPT
BANTAM DOUBLEDAY DELL DIRECT
PO BOX 985
HICKSVILLE NY 11802-9827

NO POSTAGE
NECESSARY
IF MAILED
IN THE
UNITED STATES

She whirled back to face him. "No, you're not. I am."

He put his hands on his hips and gazed broodingly at her. "I'm a great deal better than I was those first couple of nights, and I've put you out enough. The couch will be fine for me. You need to sleep in your own bed."

"Don't be silly. This couch is way too short for you. You would never be able to get comfortable enough to sleep."

"I'll be fine. Don't worry about me."

A simple request, she reflected, but one that was apparently impossible for her to give in to. He was her only concern. He had filled up her already full life, and now she couldn't begin to imagine what she would do with herself when he was gone. The mere thought of never seeing him again sent chills through her. And she was still hot. Maybe for the first time in her life she was getting sick. "I'm taking the couch."

"I thought you said we were going to work the sleeping arrangements out."

His low, husky voice lapped against her skin like heated silk. Her pulse was erratic; her ability to breathe had become impaired. She was falling apart, and she couldn't seem to help herself. "We just have, and it's settled."

"No—"

Suddenly, something snapped in her. "Dammit, it's *my* house, you're *my* guest, and you'll do what I say."

He slipped his hands into the pockets of his slacks. "My, my. Who would have thought it? An angel with a temper."

"Dammit, stop referring to me as an angel! Get past the way I look. I'm flesh and blood, Nicholas. I don't have wings. I don't have a halo. Do you have any idea how *boring* it is to be treated like an angel instead of a woman?"

He took a step closer to her. "Angel?"

"*What?*"

"Do you want me to treat you like a woman?"

"Yes!" she blurted out before she could think. "Isn't that just what I *said*? I'm not an angel. I'm a woman!" It was only then that she realized the implication of what she had said. "I didn't mean . . ."

"What exactly *did* you mean, Angel?"

"I . . ." *She had meant exactly what she had said.* The knowledge hit her with all the force, shock, and instantaneousness of a lightning bolt. She wanted him, and more than that, she *loved* him. The admission nearly stole her breath. She needed to get away from him, be by herself, and come to terms with what this new, incredible, impossible love meant to her. Because one thing she did know—the love she felt was not reciprocated.

But there was no chance that she could slip away; Nicholas was waiting for an answer, looking at her with eyes that were almost black. With passion. "I want you," she said slowly, "to treat me like a woman."

He let out a long, uneven breath, unintentionally revealing the conflicts that warred within him. " can't," he said, his voice vibrating with suppressed emotion. "It's not safe for me, and it's not safe for you." He spun on his heels so that he didn't have t look at her, didn't have to see those soft, full lips, those eyes that promised heaven. "I can't."

She stared at his back, half-angry, half-disbelieving. "This can't be that difficult, Nicholas. I'm not asking you to take me to bed, just treat me—"

He turned back, his expression bleak. "I can't."

"You can't treat me like a woman? I don't understand—"

"I just can't, that's all. I can't." He plowed his fingers through his hair. "Dammit! I *have* to." His hands shot out, reaching for her; he pulled her into his arms and brought his mouth down on hers.

Her heart, her mind, her senses, instantly opened. She loved him; it was so wonderful. She wanted him; it was so simple. And, she realized with amazement, she *had* been asking him to make love to her.

"You're going to be sorry," he muttered hoarsely against her lips, grasping the zipper in the back of her dress and sliding it down.

His tongue rasped against hers with a sensual abrasion that made the already smoldering fire within her flare and burn hot. She might be badly hurt, she thought, but she would never be sorry. "No, I won't."

He pushed the dress off her shoulders and down around her hips, exposing her upper body and the silky blue chemise she wore. Brushing a trembling hand across the top of her breasts, he groaned. "Dear Lord, this is never going to work."

She reached up and placed her hands on either side of his face. "For tonight it will."

If possible, his eyes seemed to grow even darker. "Yes, for tonight it damn sure will. It has to, or I may not survive." He lifted her into his arms and carried her down the hall to the bedroom. He felt a tugging soreness in his left side, but he ignored it. Nothing was going to stop him. Only he and Angel and what was about to happen between them were important.

She curled her arms around his neck and nestled herself against his powerful chest. Up to now, she had been like a lily floating on a clear, smooth pond. But since Nicholas had come into her life, the calm waters of her lily pond had been whipped into storm-tossed waves. Nicholas was a turbulent force, and she had the sense to know that from this point on, tranquillity would elude her.

She had made her decision, though, and she was unafraid.

In the bedroom he set her on her feet, and she stepped out of the dress and her shoes. The floor lamp was on, and its light cast a luster onto the blue chemise and panties, a gilt onto the satin of her skin. "I'll be gentle," he murmured.

She laughed, the sound as soft as moonlight. "I'm not like one of those porcelain angels on the shelf. I won't break."

"But *I* may." He slid his hands down her back to the delectable roundness of her hips and up again, then eased her into a sitting position on the side of the bed. He was trembling and as eager as a schoolboy, but he couldn't hurry. Kneeling in front of her, he lifted her foot and pressed a kiss to the inside part of her ankle, then the outside.

She inhaled sharply. "What are you doing?"

"I'm beginning," he said hoarsely, laying a line of kisses down the top of her foot to her toes.

His breath was hot against her skin, his tongue teasing. "Beginning what?"

"I'm beginning the process of learning you inch by inch." He kissed her instep, then forged a trail with his lips up her leg to the softness of her inner thigh. There he nibbled gently, seductively, erotically.

Angel moaned. Fire had followed the trail his mouth had taken, and now her lower body felt heavy, achy. Feelings such as these were all so new to her. They were at once scorchingly languorous and blazingly urgent. She felt spectacularly alive and meltingly sensual. There couldn't be anything more wonderful. . . .

His fingers pulled aside the lace edges of her panties, and his tongue flicked inside. Her heart slammed against the wall of her chest. A shock of heat jolted through her, and a new, twisting, knotting kind of tension began to build in her. She put her hands behind her to support herself and let her head fall back; her blond mane fell in a shining cascade down to the bed.

Sensation after hot sensation flooded her. Helplessly, she tangled her fingers through the thickness of his hair. Every stroke of his tongue sent a quiver through her that took her higher and higher toward a realm where rapture awaited; she couldn't bear the thought of him stopping. But abruptly he moved away from her and switched his attention to the other foot, and the new kisses sent heat racing up her leg.

He was hard and hurting; blood pounded in his

head. He had no idea from where his patience was coming. His resistance to her and his willpower were things of the past. But tasting every inch of her was his goal, learning every curve and valley his plan. His breathing turned labored as he inched his way up her thigh to once more probe the delicate, sensitive area that lay hidden behind her panties.

"Nicholas . . ."

It was almost beyond his power to cease what he was doing. But slowly, with effort, he pulled back and gazed up at her. "What?"

Her mind was blissfully blank. She couldn't think of what she had been going to say. "I don't know."

He laughed huskily. "It doesn't matter. I'm not through. You're incredible inside and out, and I've only begun." He came up on his knees, gripped the hem of the chemise, and lifted it over her head.

A stunned breath escaped from him. Her breasts were perfectly shaped, firm, and high; her stiffened nipples a delicate rose color. "Good Lord, you are so beautiful." He leaned forward and drew a nipple into his mouth, pulling on the tiny bud, worrying it, sucking the sweet honey flavor of her deep inside him. Taking her other breast into his hand, he fondled and shaped, learning the feel of her as well as her taste.

He groaned as raw need ripped through him. Desire was already clawing at him; what was he doing still dressed? He wanted to be naked, to be on top of her, in her. Fire was scorching every cell of his body. But the taste and feel of her breasts were unbelievably exciting to him, and he couldn't abandon them just yet. Each time he drew on her nipple, a thrill vibrated through him, shaking him, destroying him in the most exhilarating way. After days of wanting her, it was like a drug to be able to at last touch and kiss her anywhere and anyhow he chose.

She was burning up inside, throbbing with desire, hurting with passion. Frustration and need boiled in her. She wanted, needed, more, much more. "Nicholas!"

Her cry pierced the delirium of his mind and needed no explanation. His control broke. He jerked to his feet and hastily stripped off his clothes; then, in one smooth sweep, he took off her panties.

He moved over her and between her legs. They were skin against skin, heartbeat against heartbeat, heat against heat.

The strain of holding back had taken its toll on him. His muscles quivered, his skin gleamed with a fine sheen of sweat, his mind had almost ceased functioning. Supporting himself on his forearms, he looked down into the fathomless blue depths of her eyes. "I can't stop now."

"I thought you knew," she whispered. "I don't want you to."

The penetration was quick, the pain sharp but brief. Her body stretched to receive him, and he filled her completely, exactly, as if they had been made to fit each other.

Her fingers pressed into his back as she arched up to him. Each thrust he made created streaks of pure fire inside her, at the same time that a shimmering, feverish tension steadily grew in her lower body. With a gasp of ecstasy she wrapped her legs around his hips, giving herself to him as much as she could. She loved him, and she craved the rapture she knew he could bring her.

He plunged into her faster, harder. His need for her was powerful, primitive, and beyond his experience; the pleasure was immense and all-consuming. Knowing he couldn't hold off his completion much longer, he slipped his hand between them and stroked her, then captured her sounds of passion with his mouth, unbearably stimulated by them. Suddenly, she stiffened, and he felt her contractions begin, gently squeezing him, not so gently driving him beyond sanity.

Gripped by a savageness he had never known, he raised up and pumped powerfully into her, once, twice, and a third time. Then his own body convulsed, and violent shudders racked him as he emptied himself into her.

And all the while he held her tightly. She was his salvation, delivering him from fear, grief, anger, and pain. She was a woman who was capable of taking him to heaven.

Sometime in the night Nicholas heard the rain start. Angel was snuggled against him, her hair swirled onto his chest. He lifted a lock and sifted it through his fingers. Even in the room's dim light, the strands glistened. Her head lay on his shoulder, her breasts pressed against his side, one leg rested over his. *His angel.*

But, no . . .

He eased away from her, slid out of bed, and

went into the living room to shut the windows. Back in bed, and without intending to, he pulled her to him again and gently combed her hair from her face with his fingers. Their intense lovemaking had exhausted his body, but he hadn't been able to sleep. His mind was too active. "Angel?"

"Ummm?"

"Are you asleep?"

"I was."

"Did I hurt you?"

She laughed softly. "I was going to ask you the same thing."

Even half-asleep, she could still laugh, he thought with wonder. "I'm fine."

"What about your bruises?"

"There was no pain." The statement, he thought, said a lot. Listening to the rain as it drummed on the roof and pattered against the windows, he wondered why he had awakened her. Why had he felt as if he wanted to hear her voice? He glanced up at the angels on the shelf; they were all smiling. But then they always smiled. Didn't they?

She shifted her head so that she could gaze up at him. "Can't you sleep?"

He twined his fingers through hers and lifted her hand up for his inspection. It was small, her fingers slim and tapered, but he had seen for himself how capable those hands were. She fixed broken things, but she couldn't fix him. And he couldn't allow himself to break her. "Tonight shouldn't have happened."

"It had to, didn't it?"

Why couldn't he have as clear an understanding about things as she did? he wondered.

She raised up on one elbow, causing her hair to slide over her shoulder and cover one breast. "Your conscience should be perfectly clear about what happened between us, Nicholas." She smiled and touched a finger to his cheek. "I'm the one who shouldn't be able to sleep."

His gaze dropped to her lips, and he was surprised to feel hunger in him again. "Why's that?"

"I just made love to a man who doesn't love me."

Her words jarred him. He reached over and curved one hand over her jaw. "You haven't fallen in love with me, have you?"

She shook her head, dislodging his hand and flinging her hair back behind her shoulders. "And what if I have?" She infused the question with idle curiosity and prayed he didn't realize she had just given him an affirmative answer.

"Don't. Don't fall in love with me. I'm all broken up inside, and to make matters worse, I may not live too much longer."

"Nicholas—"

"Listen to me, Angel. I have nothing to offer you nothing to give."

"Have I asked for anything?"

"Baby, just looking at you almost demands a commitment."

"And you look at me all the time."

He pulled his gaze from her and stared straight ahead. "I know."

"You're wrong, Nicholas."

"Yes, for you."

"That's not what I meant."

He sighed. "You want to hear something funny? All my life I've avoided serious entanglements with women. Like I said before, you have to be alone in the cockpit."

She could try to convince him he was wrong, but she would lose in the end. The philosophy was too ingrained in him. She loved him, but she had no illusions about him loving her. "Okay, so what is it that's so funny?"

"It's just that now all I can think about is getting tangled up with you again until we can't tell where you begin and I end."

"I don't think that's funny. I think it's a wonderful idea." She leaned over him and pressed a kiss along his jawline.

He turned his face and caught her lips for a brief, fiery moment, but then abruptly drew back. "There's more," he said, troubled, angry. "All my life I've been in a hurry. Now all I want to do is stay here in this peaceful little town and be with you."

"I don't see a problem," she said huskily. "Stay. Stay, and get tangled up with me."

He slowly rolled his head on the pillow and gazed at her. Her skin was luminescent, her lips sexily swollen, the tips of her breasts stiff and beckoning. A low, gruff sound rumbled up from his chest, and he reached for her. "For now I'll stay. I can't seem to do anything else."

Nicholas was still asleep when Angel awoke. As quietly as possible, she slipped from the bed and dressed in jeans and a T-shirt. In the kitchen she set a pot of coffee to brew, then went to the back door and greeted Larry, Moe, and Curly. They had learned to wait at the kitchen door in the mornings, listening for noises that would signal she was up. She gave each dog a big hug, fed them, then took a cup of coffee out to the front porch.

The rain had stopped, leaving the air sparkling and clean. A west wind was blowing, warm and gentle, bringing with it the faint tangy smell of the ocean and the fragrant scent of wild aster, laurel, and rhododendron. She sat on the porch railing, sipped her coffee, and smiled. It was a gorgeous, glorious day, and she was going to spend it with Nicholas.

That he didn't love her, that he was in danger and would soon leave, threatened to overwhelm her radiant mood, like dark, heavy clouds. But she was going to do her best not to allow the shadows to block out the day's sunshine.

A car turned into her driveway, and pulled to a stop behind her car.

Jane climbed out, crossed the yard, and mounted the steps to the porch. "Good morning."

"What are you doing out and about so early?"

"It's not that early, Angel. It's"—she checked her watch—"nine-thirty."

"Oh." From the moment Nicholas had pulled her into his arms, she had lost track of time. "Want some coffee?"

"No, thanks. I've had my quota." Keeping an assessing eye on her, Jane dropped down onto the glider and sent it moving back and forth with push of her foot. "I came to see how you survived the night."

She couldn't play coy. Not with Jane. "You're not referring to the rainstorm, are you?"

"Uh-uh. There was a considerable amount of tension between you and Nicholas last night at the pub that was really interesting, to say the least."

"Yeah, well, he's an interesting man. And . . ."

"And?"

Angel shrugged. "I've fallen in love with him."

Jane's expression turned to wonder. "I almost can't believe it. Matthew said you didn't seem yourself yesterday, but it never once occurred to me that you might have fallen in love."

Angel chuckled ruefully. "It didn't occur to me either until last night. But something was bothering me all day yesterday. I couldn't even fix anything. Now I know what the trouble was. My heart was trying to tell me something, and I wasn't listening."

"Matthew said he thought all your gears were gummed up."

Angel laughed. "Don't you just love the way he throws his medical knowledge around?"

"You know," Jane said, continuing with her own train of thought, "I was beginning to wonder if I would ever see this day. You've kept your heart untouched for all these years, and then suddenly a complete stranger comes along, crashes through your fence and into your tree—"

"And right into my heart."

"Exactly." Jane clapped her hands. "Well, I couldn't be happier for you. I think it's great!"

When Angel didn't say anything, her glee slowly faded. "Isn't it great?"

Angel gazed down at her coffee cup. "It is for me. And it is for now."

"For now?" Jane's mouth dropped open with incredulity. "Are you telling me he doesn't love you? Is he *crazy*?"

"No, he's just got a whole other life somewhere else."

Jane gasped. "Oh, my Lord, he's not married, is he? He said he wasn't. He wasn't lying to me, was he?"

Humor tugged at the corners of Angel's mouth. "No. He's not married."

"Well, *that's* certainly a relief." She fanned herself with her hand. "So then what's the problem? And what's with this whole-other-life nonsense? When people fall in love, the procedure is to join their lives and become one, so to speak."

"You never did."

"I never fell in love. I had other priorities, as you very well know. Now quit changing the subject. I want to know why Nicholas isn't in love with you."

Angel grinned. "You sound as if he's breaking some sort of law by not being in love with me. This is America. He has the right not to love me if he doesn't want to."

Jane gave a snort of disgust. "I don't remember reading that anywhere in the Bill of Rights."

"Nevertheless—"

Jane sternly pointed one finger at Angel. "He had better not hurt you, or he'll have to answer to me."

Angel set her coffee mug on the railing, walked to the glider, and bent to give her a hug. "Thank you for caring, but I'm very happy now. And when he leaves, I'll pick up my life where it was before he came into it and go on as best I can. I'll be all right." Straightening, she said a silent prayer that she was right. Her heart understood the decision she had made; her mind had grave misgivings.

Jane stood. "I don't like this, but there doesn't appear to be anything I can do about the situation. Of course, I could have a good heart-to-heart with Nicholas."

Angel linked her arm with Jane's and guided her down the steps to her car. "That's a really bad idea. Why don't we forget that one?"

"Yeah, I suppose." At the car Jane turned to her. "Listen, I'll stay out of this because I guess I have to, but if you need me, call."

"Don't I always?"

Jane nodded and opened the car door. "Oh, I almost forgot. Last night's rain just about did my old roof in. When can you get over and put on a new one?"

"As soon as Nicholas leaves."

"When do you think that will be?"

"Unfortunately, I have a feeling it will be soon."

From the bedroom window, Nicholas watched Angel and Jane embrace, then Jane get in her car and back out of the driveway. He returned to the bed, propped himself up against a pile of pillows, and reached for the cup of coffee he had placed on the bedside table.

Angel stuck her head in the door. "You're awake!"

"I woke up, heard you and Jane out on the porch, and decided to have a shower." He gestured to the towel that lay across his lap.

She had already noticed the towel. More than that, she had noticed the areas of his body the towel *didn't* cover. His masculinity was overpowering and made her throat tighten. "You heard Jane and me?"

"I heard your voices, not what you said." One dark brow lifted. "Should my ears be burning?"

She smiled. "No, not really."

He patted the space beside him. "Come sit down and tell me what 'No, not really' means."

With a laugh she settled herself beside him, facing him. She rested her hand on his chest and allowed her fingers to brush back and forth over the still-moist silky black hair. "Jane came by to chat, that's all."

"That's not all. She's concerned about you, isn't she? I could see it in her face right before she left. I'm sure she's ready for you to kick me out."

She leaned toward him and pressed a light kiss to his mouth. "Well, if she is, she's out of luck."

"You should, you know."

She searched her mind for something she could say to distract him. "She came over to see when I can put a new roof on her house."

"You roof houses?" he asked in amazement.

"On occasion."

"Tell Jane to get someone else to do it."

Now it was her turn to be amazed. "Why?"

"It's too dangerous."

She would like to think his anxiety over her safety was because he cared deeply for her, but she knew it was a natural reaction. A lot of people who didn't know her well thought it wasn't a woman's place to be crawling around on a roof with a hammer and a pack of shingles. "It's not dangerous if you know what you're doing, and I do. End of discussion."

His lips quirked. "How can someone who looks as delicate as a piece of Meissen china be so—"

Her eyes alight with laughter, she put her hand over his mouth. "Careful what you say." He mumbled something. "What?"

He grasped her wrist and pulled her hand away. "Sexy. I was going to say 'be so sexy.'"

She burst out laughing. "Yeah, sure you were."

He groaned. "Sometimes I don't know which is worse. Your eyes, your smile, or your laugh. You devastate me, did you know that?"

She could make him want her, but she couldn't make him love her. But he was with her now, and if now was all she was going to have, she wanted to make the best of it. She delved her hand into his chest hair so that it curled around her fingers. Then she bent her head to his nipple and delicately used her tongue to elicit a moan from him.

Gripping her arms, he shifted her so that she lay lengthwise on top of his body. Then he cupped her buttocks and ground her pelvis against his. "Why are you dressed?"

She smiled down at him. "I'll take care of the situation immediately, if you'll let me up."

His lips quirked. "That sounds like a catch-22. I'm damned if I do and damned if I don't."

She moved her hips seductively. "It's a problem, all right."

"What the hell," he muttered, pulling her mouth down to his. "We'll work it out."

Eight

Larry, Moe, and Curly ran happily up and down the beach, barking excitedly at any sea gull that happened to swoop too low. When the dogs weren't colliding, they were tripping or stumbling over one another.

Sitting above the tide line with Angel, Nicholas was enjoying the sight, along with the warmth of the sun and the soothing sound of the ocean. "Their grace doesn't improve on sand, does it?" he said dryly.

She laughed. "I guess the stove in my workshop and the beach run neck and neck as their favorite places. I bring them down here with me every time I come."

As always, her laughter drew his gaze. The wind had tossed shining blond strands across her face. He reached over and gently tucked them behind her ear. "Were they with you when I nearly hit you?"

She nodded. "They were behind me and hadn't started across the road yet." She saw a muscle jerk along his jaw. "What's wrong?"

He shook his head to rid himself of the vision of her in the center of the road, completely unprotected, as his car hurtled toward her. "I get vaguely ill every time I think of how close I came to killing you."

"Yeah, well, I get the same feeling every time I remember that someone nearly killed you." She tucked her arm in his. "Have you had any more thoughts on who it might be?"

He was silent for a moment, his eyes fixed on the undulating ocean and the horizon beyond. She followed his gaze and saw *real* clouds gathering there; the peace of the day would not last.

"The brake line had to have been shaved at Jazz's funeral," he said at last. "That means it was either someone who was there to attend the service, or . . ."

"Or?"

"Or else it was someone who knew I would be there. If that's the case, that person stayed out of sight until we were in the house after the service, paying our respects to Jazz's parents, and then shaved the line."

She frowned. "That doesn't help narrow down the suspects one bit. The field still seems pretty much wide open."

He absently patted her hand that was curved around his arm. "You're right."

"Then start with the people at the funeral. What about Jazz's family? Do you think they blamed you for his death?"

Nicholas shook his head. "Strangely enough, they don't. They understood his need to fly, and they knew how much the project meant to him, to *all* of us, for that matter."

"I suppose the family of a pilot would have to understand the pilot's need to fly. Otherwise they'd go crazy with worry."

"I don't know. I've always been on the other side of the worry, the guy up in the plane instead of the guy on the ground. Up to now, that is." Self-contempt underscored the last statement. He lurched to his feet, took a few steps away from her, and thrust his hands into his pockets.

She contemplated the rigidity of his back. "You know, I used to close myself off when something happened that I couldn't control, exactly the way you did just now."

He looked back over his shoulder, a scowl on his face. "What are you talking about?"

"Talking about flying touched a nerve in you, so you got up, turned your back on me, and effectively closed yourself off from me."

He turned around. "What I did, Angel, was get up to stretch my legs."

"And at the same time you did what I said. You closed yourself off from me."

He gave a sound of disgust. "Why would I do that?"

"Because I'd brought up a subject that made you remember something you don't want to think about anymore, the subject of you as a pilot."

"Don't start analyzing me, Angel."

"It's not analysis. I *know* what I'm talking about, because I remember all too well when I was little, how alone and frightened I felt when I closed myself off from a situation I had no control over. And, Nicholas, you're reacting just as I did back then."

Annoyed, but nevertheless curious, he came down beside her. "Why did you feel alone and frightened? Where was Jane?"

"She was there. As head of the orphanage, it was her responsibility to try to get the orphans adopted. And guess what? I was her number-one star orphan. I was blond, blue-eyed, and more important, young."

A frown appeared between his brows. "I thought she loved you. Why would she want to get rid of you?"

"She didn't want to, but as I said, it was her job, and she felt that if she could find a couple who could give me a better life, then it was her duty to do so."

"What did she view as a better life?"

"You know. A nice, stereotypical home where there was both a mother and father."

"What happened?"

"Over the years there were a lot of couples who came to the orphanage. Practically without exception, they would take one look at me and decide they wanted me."

"Obviously, they didn't take you."

"No. I might have been young, but I understood what they were doing, and the idea of leaving the only home I had ever known frightened me to death. So I would stiffen up, close myself off, freeze them out, and refuse to talk to them. And in the end every one of them said, 'Thank you, but no thank you.' They wanted a child who was adorable and cuddly, not one who wouldn't even look at them."

"Did Jane understand what you were doing?"

She nodded. "Yes, and seeing me so frightened almost broke her heart. Years later she told me that she kept thinking I would grow out of the tendency to freeze the prospective parents out, and that once I did, she would find me a wonderful home to go to. But one day she couldn't take it anymore. After yet another couple had left, she pulled me onto her lap and told me she would never again put me through another one of those interviews. In effect, she labeled me unadoptable."

His gaze was thoughtful. "So your instinct was to be still until the threat went away, and it worked."

"Yes."

Down the beach the dogs had found a small piece of driftwood and were tossing it about. He watched them, thinking about what she had said. "You're right," he said after several minutes. "That's exactly how I've been dealing with the fact that someone wants me dead. I've been trying to be still by staying here, hoping that the threat will just go away."

"But it's not working, is it?"

"No."

"It's also how you've been dealing with your fear of flying, and as far as I can see, that's not working either."

His jaw clenched; his expression hardened. "It's not the same thing. I've accepted that I'm never going to fly again, but I am damn well going to find out who's trying to kill me."

She didn't believe that he had accepted that his life as a pilot was over, but she had something else she needed to say to him. She chose her next words carefully. "Remember when you told me that you and your friends were being grounded one by one? That of the five of you, only Blare was still flying?"

"Yes," he said, his tone bleak. "I remember."

"Has it occurred to you that whoever is trying to kill you might be responsible for not only the deaths of Rocky and Jazz, but also Hawk's accident?"

He slowly turned toward her, astonishment on his face. "No, it hasn't."

She shrugged. "I think it's a theory worth considering."

He rubbed his forehead to clear his mind. "*Damn*, why haven't I thought of that before?"

"Because you've been too busy trying to deal with your grief, plus trying to save your project."

"Still—"

"You've got to quit blaming yourself for everything, Nicholas."

Unexpectedly, he chuckled. "It's no wonder I don't want to leave this place. You absolve me of all my guilt."

"It's not up to me to forgive you, Nicholas. It's up to you."

With a sigh he attempted to regain his humor. "It's too bad you have this one really annoying habit of trying to fix me."

"You seem to have a lot about you that needs

fixing," she said, smiling to let him know she was teasing.

He didn't need to see the smile; her eyes were alight with humor, warming all the cold, empty spots inside him. It was no wonder he kept putting off leaving. "If you can change me, you will have performed a miracle. And since you insist you're not an angel, I don't think you'll have much of a chance."

There wasn't anything she could say to that since she happened to agree with him. "Okay, then, let's get back to Jazz's funeral. The new theory rules out the families of Jazz and Rocky, and anyway, you're pretty certain that they don't hold a grudge against you. Right?"

"Right."

"Okay, then, who else was at the funeral?"

"Hawk and Blare."

"Do you trust them?"

"With my life."

"That's exactly what we're talking about here, Nicholas. And one of those two men is grounded and the other isn't."

"There's no way that it's Blare. You couldn't get me to believe that in a million years."

"For your sake, I hope you're right, and unfortunately that puts us back to where we started. We still don't know who's trying to kill you."

We, she had said. As if they were irrevocably joined as one. And at that moment he couldn't imagine not being with her. But their time together was getting shorter and shorter. . . .

The sound of a military jet flying high above

them drew his gaze, and he followed it as it streaked across the sky.

She watched his expression turn from contemplative to incalculably sad in a matter of seconds. "If flying means that much to you, Nicholas, you'll fly again, because you have to."

He couldn't tear his gaze from the jet. He had flown the same type many times, and he was filled with envy for the pilot, knowing the freedom and the absolute exhilaration the pilot was feeling. He felt as if he had been halved in two, with the absence of flying leaving him less than whole. But there was simply nothing he could do about it.

When he could no longer see the jet, he turned to her. "Don't you think I'd fly if I could? I've tried, but I couldn't even make myself climb into the cockpit. Just the thought had me breaking out in a cold sweat. I've lost my nerve and my courage. And, dammit, stop looking at me like that."

"Like what?"

"Like I'm a bird with a broken wing. You can't fix me, Angel. Don't even bother trying."

She held up her hands, showing him that her hands were idle. "I'm not doing anything."

"Angel, you're doing something by merely *existing*."

"Like what?" she asked, puzzled.

He flexed his hands, suddenly realizing he was very uptight. But then again, he supposed his tension was understandable. Since they had been on the beach, he had practically run the gamut of emotions. He took a deep breath, forcing himself to relax. "Oh, you don't do things that are really big," he said wryly. "Just things like altering my thought processes and making me want you until I'm almost crazy with it."

She hid her grin of happiness. "Oh, is that all. For a minute there, I thought it was something serious."

He laughed. "Come on. Those clouds out there are starting to roll in, but we have a little time before it starts raining. Let's go into town."

"What for?"

"To do some grocery shopping. I'm going to make dinner tonight."

"You cook?"

"In a strictly limited way."

"How limited?"

"I can grill steaks, and I can make spaghetti. Tonight I'm going to make spaghetti."

Thunder rumbled in the distance. Angel glanced out the window and saw Larry, Moe, and Curly scurrying into the workshop through the doggy door. She turned back to Nicholas. "Are you sure you don't want any help?"

"I've got everything under control," he said, adding more garlic to the sauce.

He had a frown of concentration on his face, but she had the feeling that the sauce hadn't caused the intensity of his expression. Somehow she knew he had made his decision about when he would leave, and she guessed it would be tomorrow.

She wrapped her arms around herself, fighting a sudden chill that had nothing to do with the approaching storm. Her instinct was to draw away from him, as he seemed to be withdrawing from her.

The signs were subtle. On the surface he wasn't acting differently, but she sensed a new tension in the way he held himself, and in the almost imperceptible distance in his eyes.

He emptied a pack of spaghetti into a pot of boiling water, then glanced over at her. "I need to apologize to you for something."

"What?"

"I haven't used any form of birth control, and I'm truly sorry about that." His mouth tightened, and he shook his head. "Being here with you has seemed like an interval and place out of time, but that's no excuse."

The strength in her legs gave out, and she sank to the nearest chair. He sounded as if he was trying to settle his account with her. Except she had never considered there was an account, just love, at least on her part. "Don't worry about it."

"I want you to know that you have nothing to be concerned about regarding any type of disease."

Again she wrapped her arms around herself, trying to fight the temptation to seal herself away from this analytical discussion of what she had regarded as lovemaking. And from him.

"But there is the possibility of a baby."

He didn't have to spell it out for her. A baby would be a responsibility, and right or wrong, he had very definite reasons for avoiding emotional ties. "There won't be a problem. It's the wrong time of the month for me to conceive."

The look of relief on his face tore at her heart. She hadn't been truthful with him, but she couldn't bear for him to feel responsible for her in any way. If she had a baby, he would stay against his will, and that would be worse than him not staying at all.

Nicholas fished a strand of spaghetti from the pot and tossed it against the wall in front of him to test its degree of doneness. But he stared unseeingly at it. In his mind he saw a little girl with blond hair and blue eyes, as angelic as her mother. *His* child. A fierce, powerful emotion gripped him. What in the hell was wrong with him? He had never wanted a child. His future had never been more uncertain, and instead of living on the edge of danger as he had in the past, he felt as if he had gone right over the edge.

He fished out a couple more strands of spaghetti and tossed them against the wall just as a big clap of thunder sounded and Matthew walked in the door.

He glanced at Angel, then at Nicholas, then back at Angel. "About to come a big storm."

Jane had told him that she was in love with Nicholas, Angel thought, and he had come to see for himself how she was. "So what are you doing here? You should be home."

"I've just come from Mrs. Reynolds. She was eager to tell me the new cure she's discovered for her arthritis. Claims that sticking needles in all the eyes of a potato and burying it in the backyard at midnight has cured her."

"What did you say to her?" Nicholas asked.

He shrugged. "I congratulated her on her cure. If she thinks it works, it works." He eyed the spaghetti on the wall with interest. "Looks like a Picasso drawing. Are you an artist, Nicholas?"

He grinned. "No, and I'm not much of a cook, but I've made a lot of this, and you're welcome to join us for dinner."

Matthew rubbed his hands together. "Good thing you asked, or I was going to have to invite myself. I'm starved. Mrs. Reynolds only had petits fours to offer me. So, Angel, have you fixed my fan yet?"

"I haven't been back out at the shop since yesterday, but you'll have it soon."

"Think you'll be able to fix it now?"

"I know so."

"Mm-hmmm."

Matthew left right after dinner, and Angel couldn't help but breathe a sigh of relief. She now knew how it felt to be inspected under a microscope. And strangely enough, Nicholas had seemed to be studying her as thoroughly as Matthew.

She carried their dishes to the counter where Nicholas was filling the sink with soapy water. She accidentally brushed her arm against him as she was setting down the plates, and she instinctively recoiled. Self-protection was a strong, basic instinct, she thought ruefully.

"Are you feeling all right?" asked Nicholas, his brow creased.

"I'm fine. Why?"

"You seemed unusually quiet during dinner."

"Matthew talks to me all the time. I figured he'd

enjoy talking to someone new, and I was right. He had a great time."

His mouth quirked wryly. "He's easily entertained. If someone doesn't amuse him, he entertains himself by telling some of those awful jokes of his."

Silently, she returned to the table for the rest of the dishes, then eased them into the soapy water.

"Angel?"

Instead of answering, she glanced absently toward the windows and saw the rain coming down in earnest. He shut off the water, turned, and leaned his hips against the counter. "You're doing it, aren't you?"

She blinked. "Excuse me?"

"You're trying to close me out. Why?"

Because I love you, and it's going to hurt so much when you leave. "You're mistaken."

"Uh-uh." He pulled her in front of him, then linked his hands at the back of her waist, locking her against him. "You were right today. Once you know the signs, they're unmistakable. So why, Angel? What have I done?"

She stared at his chin, unwilling to look into his eyes, unsure if she wanted to see the color of dark jade or the color of passion, black. "You're leaving, aren't you?"

"You always knew I would."

"Yes, but you've decided to leave tomorrow, haven't you?" It was thirty-nine seconds before she heard him speak again. She knew, because she counted each one of them.

"It's time for me to go," he said quietly. "I have to

face whatever, or whoever, is back at home waiting for me."

Unable to help herself, she lifted her head and met his gaze. Jade. "But it won't be safe for you. You still don't know who the enemy is."

"If I could have figured it out here, Angel, I would have by now."

Then take me with you, she pleaded silently, not daring to say the words out loud. She smiled. "Then I guess you've made the right decision." She broke away from his hold and went back to the table, busying herself by straightening the chairs.

He had never seen her force a smile, and he wished he hadn't now. *Dammit.* Parting from her shouldn't be this hard! But it was. Seeing her attempting to seal herself off from him shouldn't tear him up inside. But it did. "I'm not going to let you do this, Angel."

"You can take my car if you like. Whit keeps several cars in running condition so his customers can have something to drive while he's working on their cars. I'm sure he'll let me borrow one."

Her words were addressed to him, but she wasn't talking to him, he thought grimly, nor was she paying any attention to what she was saying. And with every word she spoke, fury grew in him.

"Or now that I think about it, you could use one of his. Maybe that would be better. You can return his car when you come to pick yours up. You won't waste time that way. In the morning you can call him—"

In the space of a heartbeat he crossed to her and

hauled her into his arms. "*Stop.* Just stop. I'm not going to let you shut me out my last night here."

Her face was without expression. "Does it matter?"

"Yes, dammit, it does. I need you. I haven't had enough of you yet. You're still in my head and—"

She pulled away from him. "And you've got to get me out," she said, her voice louder and harder than he had ever heard it. "Right, Nicholas? Because you need all your wits to be as sharp as they can be, and if you were thinking about me, you might slip and not react to the danger as fast as you should. Right? Okay, then. I agree. I think you're absolutely correct in your thinking. What's more, I'm going to help you." She whirled and started for the door. "I'll make up the couch for you—"

He caught her before she could reach the door and spun her around and up against the wall, then pushed his pelvis against hers. "No!" he muttered thickly. "We're both going to be in your bed tonight, because that's the way it's got to be."

She closed her eyes, willing herself to ignore the passion in his voice. But then she felt his mouth on the side of her neck, and heat started in her belly and began spreading down into her lower body.

He laid down a necklace of kisses around her neck, long kisses, hot kisses. At the same time, he drew down the zipper of her dress and smoothed his hand inside to the softness of her skin. "Let's make the most of the time we have left," he said huskily, and claimed her mouth.

With each caress, with each thrust of his tongue, her control weakened. His brand of sensuality was drugging, his way of making love to her impossible to resist.

He pushed his leg between hers and raised his knee beneath the dress up against her panties. Heat pooled where his knee pressed and spread to every area of her body. Against her will, her arm slid around his neck, and she moaned.

"Yes," he whispered fiercely. "Moan, cry out, tell me what you want."

Even though her body was betraying her, she was still aware that, no matter what, she had to keep him from finding out that she loved him. She didn't want to hold him to her by guilt.

She moved against his knee, and once again she moaned. The sound scorched through his brain and arrowed down to his groin, shattering his control. With a muttered curse he reached between her legs and ripped off her panties.

Elation and excitement beat in her. She knew what was about to happen, and her body was crying out for it. She drove her fingers through his hair and delved her tongue deeply into his mouth.

He unzipped his pants, releasing his hard, throbbing length, and lifted her. Quickly, she wrapped her legs around him, and then he surged into her. Fiery pleasure streaked clear up to her head, out to the tips of her fingernails, down to her toes. She squeezed her eyes shut, cried out, and held on tightly to him. His hips moved in a fast, wild, primitive rhythm, impaling her time after time until he felt something inside her explode.

"Angel," he whispered.

Then his own completion came, and he was experiencing the same thing. Powerful spasms of satisfaction rolled over and through him, measureless, boundless, limitless.

"Angel," he cried.

Nine

Nicholas's chest heaved as he struggled for both breath and strength. The utter power and force of the need he had just experienced had left him badly shaken. But though his body might be temporarily drained, his need for her had not yet been sated.

He managed to move his head slightly to look at the kitchen door and was gratified to see it was open. Without withdrawing from her, he wrapped his arms around her hips, paused long enough to switch off the light, then carried her into her bedroom.

Tightening his hold on her, he eased them both onto the bed, then rolled over so that they were side by side. "I didn't mean to let things get away from me like that," he said, smoothing her hair back from her face.

She stared at his lips, watching them move and change shape as they formed the words. If he apologized to her for one more thing, she thought, she was going to scream. "You don't have to apologize. I wasn't exactly an innocent bystander."

He chuckled. "I remember. You were magnificent." He pressed a gentle kiss to her lips, then slowly drew away from her.

Suddenly, she felt empty, and she barely stopped herself from crying out in protest and pulling him back to her. Instead she stretched lazily. "Are you ready to get some sleep?"

"Not yet. I want you again, undressed and beneath me." He stood, quickly skimmed off his own clothes, then came back down to her.

The lamp threw light and shadows over the lean, muscled length of him, and his eyes gleamed as black as coal. Her breasts began to ache, and her blood heated in anticipation of the ecstasy that was to come. But she knew she still had to be careful. So far, she had only bared her passion to him, not her love.

This time he took his time, wanting to extend the incredible, heavenly pleasure as long as he could. He stripped her of her clothes in a leisurely, seductive manner, kissing each area of her skin as it was revealed: her breasts, her midriff, her stomach, and lower. Then he turned her over so that he could give the same attention to her back. He had gotten as far as her shoulder blades when he paused.

"What are these marks here?" he asked huskily, fingering two vertical blemishes on her otherwise perfect skin, one on each of her shoulder blades. "I've noticed them before."

She stifled a sound of frustration that he had stopped. "They're scars."

"They're odd-looking scars." He chuckled softly. "They actually look like places where wings could be attached. Do you come with instructions? *Fit wings into Slot A and Slot B.*"

She groaned. "Don't start that."

"I'm serious."

She rolled onto her side and gazed at him, a frown of annoyance between her brows. "When I was a little girl, I fell out of a tree and landed on something."

"Something?" he asked, running his fingers up and down her spine.

Heat coursed where his fingers had been, and anxious for him to continue the lovemaking, she hurriedly offered the explanation. "I'm not sure what it was, but it was sharp enough to cut through my blouse and penetrate the skin. I got up and ran back to the orphanage, and after Jane cleaned me up and bandaged the wounds, we went back to the tree to see if we could find what I had fallen on."

"Did you?"

"No. There was nothing there."

He stared at her. "There is a lot about you that's unexplainable, Angel."

Good, she thought, and gasped as he began kissing her again. He must never know how much she had come to love him.

He learned her spine with his mouth, went on to the incline of her hips, and then traversed the gentle curve of her buttocks and down her legs. When he reached the soles of her feet, he switched to the other leg and made the return journey to her shoulders.

By the time he reached her neck, she was burning and mad with desire. The rain had stopped, and the only sound in the room was their breathing, shallow, quick, and more urgent with each passing second. Without his having to ask, she rolled over on her back and reached for him.

He entered her with the familiarity of a longtime lover, and almost immediately his control was overwhelmed by his passion. "Open your eyes, Angel," he said hoarsely. "Don't keep them closed like you did before. Don't shut me out. I want you to look at me when it happens. Your eyes are your soul, and I want to see all the way to heaven."

She kept her eyes tightly closed, fighting against doing as he said. A rough sound tore from his chest, and he slowed his pace, easing off on the force of his thrusts. She could feel his body shuddering beneath her hands, and then the heated intensity began to rebuild, slowly, surely, then faster, prolonging and intensifying the pleasurable agony until she was clawing at his back.

"Open your eyes, Angel."

His words, spoken in a broken rasp, demanded, commanded. She opened her eyes, and at that moment she was caught up by a wave of all-consuming rapture and was swept away.

Gripped by the fury and magnitude of his own approaching climax, Nicholas stared down into her eyes. Searching for heaven, he found it and something else.

Love.

But then a guttural cry ripped up from his chest,

and awareness vanished. Seized with the contractions of completion, he reared his head back and drove into her.

Something crashed nearby. The sound startled Nicholas out of the deep, exhausted sleep into which he had fallen. In the dim light he saw one of the porcelain angels, lying on the floor beside the bed, broken. Simultaneously, he inhaled the strong, unmistakable smell of gas. *"Angel, get up!"*

His feet hit the floor, and he grabbed for his pants.

Coughing, Angel raised up on one elbow. "What?"

He zipped up his pants, yanked her robe from the closet door, and threw it to her. "Put this on and go outside fast. The house is filled with gas. Don't turn on any lights."

Fully awake now and able to smell the gas, Angel wasted no more time asking questions. She wrapped the robe around her and followed him out of the room. "Wait," she said, reaching for his arm when he turned toward the hall that led to the kitchen. "Come this way. The front door is closer."

"You go out that way. Now! I've got to get to the kitchen to turn off the gas."

"But—"

"Don't argue! Do it!"

Without waiting to see her go, he strode down the hall, his chest burning, his eyes stinging. At the door he reached for the knob, then froze.

The door had been open when he had carried Angel to bed.

The hairs on the back of his neck stood up. He took a step back and ran right into Angel. Without offering an explanation, he took her hand and as fast as possible hurried her out of the house.

By the time they got outside, both were coughing badly. "Breathe," he said, drawing lungfuls of deep, rain-cleaned air into his system and watching her as she did the same.

When she could manage to speak without coughing, she asked, "What happened? Why didn't you go into the kitchen?"

"I could be wrong, but I think that door is rigged to cause an explosion on opening."

Her eyes widened. "You mean there isn't a gas leak?"

His jaw tightened. "Like I said, I could be wrong, but I'm going to find out." He drew one last deep breath, then reached for her hand and headed to the back of the house.

He saw the hole immediately. Someone had used a glass cutter to carve out a section of glass in the door; the hole would have given access to the lock on the inside. Several layers of heavy plastic had been taped over the hole to make sure no gas could escape that way.

"Damn!"

Angel reached out and put her free hand on his chest, acting with a blind, instinctive need to feel his heartbeat and confirm to herself that he had made it through another murder attempt.

Breaking away, he tore the plastic off the door, then stopped. "I need to be careful. I still don't know what, if anything, has been rigged. Do you have a flashlight out in your workshop?"

She nodded. "I'll be right back." Her bare feet flew over the wet grass. Once inside, she turned on the light and went right to the shelf where she kept the flashlight. Then a sixth sense made her look over at the dogs. They hadn't woken up when she had come in. "Larry? Moe? Curly?"

With a cry of alarm she dropped to her knees beside them and leaned closer. They were all breathing, but they seemed to be in a heavy, drugged sleep. Someone had tranquilized them.

She gave each several loving strokes, then raced back to Nicholas.

He took the flashlight from her and beamed its light through the glass, searching the kitchen. When he didn't see anything, he returned the flashlight to her, reached through the glass, and opened the door. "Stay here until I get the gas turned off."

"Be careful, Nicholas."

He nodded and entered the house. The fumes were so strong, he almost gagged, and his eyes instantly began tearing. Quickly, he turned off all four gas jets and the oven, then turned his attention to the windows, flinging them up one after the other, letting in the cool night breeze.

He stumbled back outside, rubbing his eyes. "Let's give it a few minutes and let some of that gas out of there." His voice sounded grainy, and his chest burned. He drew in several deep breaths, then looked at Angel. "Are you all right?"

She nodded. "But I'm not sure about the dogs. They've been tranquilized."

He uttered a violent curse. "Do you have a phone out in the workshop?"

"Yes."

"Call the sheriff. Whoever it is could still be around here."

Her heart thudded against her ribs. "Then I'm not going to leave you. He may try to kill you while I'm gone."

"If that were the case, he would have made his move when you went for the flashlight." He didn't really believe that he was safe, he thought grimly as he watched her go, but he needed her to call the sheriff. He had delayed too long bringing in the law. Reflecting that the kitchen should be somewhat cleared of the gas by now, he went back in. Using the flashlight, he focused his attention on the kitchen door.

He didn't see anything, no wires of any kind, no explosive devices. He walked closer and ran the beam of light down the narrow gap between the doorjamb and the door. Nothing.

He sank to the floor, lay on his side, and did the same with the bottom of the door. It was then that he saw it.

A pack of matches had been taped to the bottom of the door, and directly beneath it a piece of sandpaper had been taped to the floor. So simple, and so effective. If he had opened the door, the matches would have struck, and the whole house would have been blown sky-high, obiterating any sign of what had set off the explosion.

"Were you right?" Angel asked quietly, behind him.

"Yes," he said, getting to his feet. "I'm afraid I was."

The smell of gas still hung in the air, but it was

no longer strong. "I think it's all right to turn on a light."

With a nod she walked to the switch and flipped it on. "I guess I should go open up the rest of the house."

"Go out the back way. We shouldn't touch the door until the sheriff arrives."

"All right." She hesitated, sensing his rage. "Nicholas?"

Her gaze was troubled, and he did his best to reassure her. "I'm all right. Go on."

She left by the back door, and in a minute he heard her opening the windows in the front of the house.

She had felt his anger, he thought, but she didn't understand the true cause. Granted he was shaken by the undisputed evidence that this faceless enemy of his hadn't given up on trying to kill him. But there was one other reason for his anger, a compelling, overmastering reason.

The danger in his life had touched her, and that he could not tolerate.

"No fingerprints," Sheriff Dobson said, having just finished dusting the doors and the surrounding areas.

He was a solidly built, portly man, and he had showed up in overalls, but Nicholas hadn't been with him more than two minutes before he realized the man had sharp eyes and a keen mind.

He fixed Nicholas with a level gaze. "Ange doesn't have an enemy in the world. That leave you, and without stretching my imagination too far, I'd say this enemy is a powerful one."

"I know," Nicholas said grimly.

The sheriff accepted a freshly brewed cup of coffee from Angel. "Did either of you see or hear anything unusual this evening?"

Nicholas exchanged a glance with Angel and saw that she was thinking the same thing he was. During their lovemaking they probably wouldn't have heard a bomb go off. Afterward, they had both slept deeply. If it hadn't been for the angel crashing to the floor . . . "No, not a thing."

The sheriff threw a glance at the back door. "A window cutter is quiet, and I'm guessing he probably parked his car some distance away and walked here. Probably brought the tranquilizers with him wrapped up in some meat, just in case he ran into any dogs. And he did."

Blare had heard the dogs barking. The sudden thought almost paralyzed Nicholas.

"How are your dogs, Angel?" Sheriff Dobson asked.

"I called the vet. He said as long as they're breathing all right, there'll be no problem. They just have to sleep it off. He'll be over in the morning to check on them."

"Good." The big man turned back to Nicholas. "Who knew you were here?"

His jaw clenched and unclenched. "I told one person, and I totally trust that person." *Blare.*

"Well, somebody found out where you are." He paused, thinking. "A stranger couldn't hang around here for long without being noticed. He had to know exactly where he was going and what he was going to do."

"He could have parked on that old road that runs behind the woods," Angel said. "Very few people use that road anymore, but it's pretty easy to find."

The sheriff nodded and sipped his coffee. "You're right. Then he could have hid out in the woods for a couple of hours and kept an eye on you."

"And when it got late enough, and he figured we were sleeping, he drugged my dogs and came into the house." Angel's voice sounded dull even to her ears, and she wrapped her arms around herself.

"Sheriff." A deputy was standing outside the door. "I found some footprints."

They filed out of the house to the backyard. Using their flashlights, they could make out a series of distinct footprints.

"That rain we had earlier has helped us out," the sheriff murmured, kneeling beside the prints and shining his flashlight on them. "These look to have been made by an average-size man's boot. Offhand I'd say the size was maybe a ten and a half or eleven. Smooth soles, no distinguishing marks. Too bad. But right now they're all we have to go on." He glanced up at his deputy. "Get some boards and mark this area off. We'll come back tomorrow for a closer look in the daylight." He stood and addressed both Angel and Nicholas. "We've done all we can for tonight. On our way home we'll patrol along that back road, but I really think this guy is long gone. In the meantime I suggest you two try to get some sleep."

Nicholas nodded. "Thank you for all your help."

The sheriff started toward his car, motioning for

his deputy to follow him, but then he stopped and turned back.

"What did you say woke you up?"

"One of Angel's angels fell to the floor and broke."

"What do you think caused it to fall?"

Angel spoke up. "I probably placed it too near the edge of the shelf the last time I dusted."

"When was that?"

"Sometime last week."

The sheriff shook his head, puzzled. "Well, all I can say is that it's a lucky thing the angel fell when it did, because if you two had continued sleeping, you both would have been dead by morning."

It might have been luck, Nicholas thought, glancing at Angel, but it was also odd as hell that it had taken that particular moment to fall.

Angel lay in bed, staring into the darkness. It was still several hours before dawn, and Nicholas lay at her side, motionless and quiet. She desperately wanted him to hold her. She needed his warmth, his strength, and to be reassured by the beating of his heart. But he didn't move, didn't touch her, didn't speak. He had completely withdrawn into himself. In essence he had already left her. She was sure he had seen the love in her eyes, and her love was a complication he didn't want.

Nicholas could tell by Angel's breathing that she wasn't asleep. She was probably too frightened to sleep, and he didn't blame her. He wished he could think of some way to comfort her, but his anger kept him from reaching out to her, anger at his faceless enemy for endangering her life, and anger at himself because he hadn't left for home as soon as he was able.

His anger was like a cold fire within him. He alternately burned and froze. All he could think about was that Angel had almost been killed. That and one other thing.

She loved him.

She hadn't told him of her love, and he knew why. She had freely and generously given herself to him, given all her sweet softness and blazing fire. In return he had put her in danger. And because it didn't seem to be in him to be able to make a long-term commitment, he would also hurt her tomorrow when he left.

He felt torn, as if someone had ripped him in two. He didn't want to go, but he couldn't stay. He couldn't bear to leave her, and he couldn't take her with him. And when he left, he could make no promises.

"I'm sorry," he said into the darkness.

Another apology, but she couldn't summon the energy to scream. "For what?"

"For everything."

A solitary tear slipped from beneath Angel's lashes and rolled down her cheek.

He slid from the bed while Angel still slept. He had known the exact moment she had finally fallen asleep, but he still hadn't been able to rest. He quickly and quietly pulled on a pair of slacks and a sweater. Afraid too much activity would wake her, he waited until he was in the kitchen to put on his shoes and socks. Then he let himself out the back door.

The sun had been up only a short time, but he could tell the day would be a warm one. He went to check on Larry, Moe, and Curly. When he knelt down beside them and softly called their names, they opened their eyes, gave a soft sound of greeting, thumped their tails weakly; then, like drowsy children who weren't ready to be awakened, they fell back to sleep. More for himself than for them, he gently stroked each one in turn, then went outside.

He paused beside the tracks the sheriff had marked off. It was bizarre, he thought. His enemy didn't have a face, but he had a boot size, and he had walked through Angel's backyard on the way to set a trap for them. With a frown he continued on until he reached the edge of the yard and the woods. He was no expert woodsman, but he didn't have to be to notice the broken limbs and twigs that marked the route the man had taken.

He turned and stared back at the house, seeing it from the viewpoint of the man as he had stood there, waiting for the lights to go out. The house was built of redwood and trimmed with cedar shingles. Its rustic and weathered appearance matched the rest of the town's architecture. He wondered if the man knew how happy he had been the short time he had been in that house. And if the man did know, he wondered if the knowledge had made the man's hate grow.

Blare. Along with everything else, the idea that Blare could be his enemy had tormented him all night long. He had told Blare Angel's name. It would have been simple to look up the address in a phone book. And Blare had heard the dogs barking.

No. He would believe the sun rose in the west and set in the east before he would believe Blare would try to harm him.

Angel appeared at the back door. He waved his hand and started toward her, but for some strange reason, when he reached the footprints, he paused again and stared down at them. There was something wrong about the prints. . . .

His heart stopped, then started again, sending blood rushing to his head where it pounded until he couldn't hear anything, see anything, feel anything.

"Nicholas, what's wrong?"

Her words reached him but didn't penetrate his mind.

"Nicholas?"

Could it be true? Had he really discovered a face for his enemy?

He felt her hand on his shoulder, and as it had since the beginning, the warmth of her touch reassured and soothed him. He turned to her and desperately fastened his gaze on her. The blue of her eyes and the heaven beyond was something he could believe in.

"You know who it is, don't you?" she asked quietly.

"Maybe. Let's go in the house."

Without a word she turned and headed toward the back door. He was like a trauma victim, she thought, and she was afraid to touch him again for fear of hurting him.

In the kitchen she immediately went to the stove to put on a fresh pot of coffee. Her concern for him overrode her need to know who the person was. So she watched the coffee perk and waited until he was ready to talk to her. Fortunately for her peace of mind, she was rewarded by a short wait.

"I think it might be Hawk."

"Your friend? Are you sure?"

"Yes. No." He rubbed the heel of his hand against one eye. "I'm pretty sure."

She sat down across the kitchen table from him. His eyes were black. With pain. "Tell me."

"It's the footprints. We couldn't really tell last night, but the right one is slightly deeper than the left one."

"You mean the weight distribution is off?"

"Yes. Slightly. After the accident the bones in Hawk's right leg never set right. As a result, he limps."

"But why would he want you dead?"

"I'm not sure," he said, anguish heavy in his tone. "We've always been best friends. Jazz and I were the closest, but Hawk, Rocky, and Blare completed our circle. It doesn't make any sense."

She reached over and touched his hand. "Think, Nicholas. There's got to be a reason. What is it that he could blame you for?"

He shook his head impatiently. "That's just it. There's nothing. . . . The only bad thing that's ever happened to Hawk was that damned accident."

"Tell me about the accident."

He sighed. "Lord, Angel, it was so stupid. It never should have happened. We were working late one night, and I needed someone to go up on a catwalk and check some rigging. It wasn't Hawk's job, but there was no one else around. I nearly went myself, but at the last minute I got involved with something, and I asked Hawk if he would mind going up and doing it. He did, and the catwalk collapsed."

He dropped his head in his hands, and Angel watched him, her heart aching. Finding out that it was Hawk was tearing him apart. "Do you think he blames you for sending him up on the catwalk?"

"I've never seen any sign that he did." He raised his head. "Hell, it never even occurred to me. If I'd gone up there, it would have happened to me."

"You said he had to go through a year's therapy. Was it rough on him?"

"It was hell, and to this day he still has pain."

"Plus the accident grounded him."

He nodded. "He was like me, flying was his life."

Angel took a deep breath. He wasn't going to like what she had to say next. "Okay, let's say that it is Hawk who's trying to kill you. Have you considered that he might have also caused the deaths of Rocky and Jazz?"

He paled. "Good Lord, no."

"When was Rocky's crash?"

"It was—" He broke off and looked at her, stunned. "It was a short time after Hawk returned to work, after his year of therapy."

"If he was responsible," she said gently, "then that means you weren't the cause of your friends' death. It wasn't your design. It was something outside your control and that you had nothing to do with."

"But *why*? Why Rocky and Jazz? They weren't even there that night the catwalk came down."

"I don't know, Nicholas."

He was silent for a moment. "There may be a way I can confirm this." He rose and went to the phone. Using his credit card, he punched out the numbers.

"Santini Aeronautics."

"Blare, it's me."

"Satan! I was wondering when we were going to hear from you. When are you coming home?"

"I'm starting back in an hour or so."

"Great."

"Hey, is Hawk around?"

"No. He said he might make it back later on today, but he didn't say for sure. Is there something you need?"

"Back? Where did he go?"

"I don't know. But he said since you had closed Lightning One down for the time being, he was going to take a little time off. He left yesterday right after I told him you had called."

"Did you tell him where I was?"

"Sure I did."

"And about the dogs barking?"

"Yes."

Nicholas fell back against the counter and put his hand on his face.

"Satan?"

He sighed. "Yeah, I'm here. All right, I want you

to listen to me very carefully and do exactly what I say. As soon as we hang up, I want you to walk out of the building, get in your car, and drive away."

"What's up?" Blare asked, his voice suddenly stripped of all its easygoing mood.

"Just listen for a minute. You're not to tell anyone where you're going. *No one*, do you understand? *No one*."

"I understand. Where do you want me to go?"

Nicholas thought fast. "Go to the downtown branch of the public library, get yourself a good book, and bury yourself in some out-of-the-way corner. I'll be there by this afternoon, and I'll explain everything then."

"I'll be there."

"Good. I'll see you as soon as I can."

He hung up the phone and looked at Angel. "I've got to go."

"You're afraid for Blare, aren't you?"

"Among other things."

When she had awakened this morning, it had been in her mind to abandon her noble attitude and beg him to stay. But she couldn't now. She pushed back her chair and stood up. "I'll make breakfast while you pack."

He nodded and reached for the phone again. "First, I need to talk to the sheriff. On the outside chance that Hawk is still in the area, I want you protected."

"Do you really think that's a possibility?"

"No. I think he's back at home, or at least on his way, but I've lost too many people I care about already. I don't want anything to happen to you. What's the number?"

She gave it to him, then went to the refrigerator for the bacon and eggs. In a roundabout way he had just said he cared about her, but her heart didn't leap with hope. As she well knew, there were degrees of caring. She cared about a great many people, but she didn't love them.

Nicholas laid his suitcase in the trunk of the car Whit had driven over and slammed the lid shut. He glanced toward the police car parked to the side of Angel's driveway, then looked back at her. "They'll keep an eye on you until I get things settled at home. You'll be safe."

Determined not to cry, she smiled bravely. "I know."

It was hard for him to look at her without drawing her into his arms and kissing her. But if he did, he knew he wouldn't want to leave her, at least not today. Her hair outshone the sunshine, her eyes were bluer than the sky. She had to be the loveliest of God's creations. And he had to leave her. "I have no choice, Angel."

With her smile fixed firmly in place, she shrugged. "Then go."

Her smile lacerated him. There were words he felt he needed to say, except he didn't know what they were, or even how to come up with them. "Hawk is obviously deranged, and he may have killed before. I have to make sure he's put away where he can't harm anyone else."

"I know. Just be careful. Oh, and be sure to have

a doctor look at those stitches in a few days. They'll be ready to come out."

"Angel—"

She held up her hand. "Please . . . don't thank me. Everything I did, I did because I wanted to. You owe me nothing, not even guilt."

"I—" He broke off and raked his hand through his hair. "This is so damned hard."

"No, it's not. Just get in the car and drive away. Do what you have to do and get on with your life. It's what I plan to do with mine."

"Angel—"

She couldn't take it anymore. If he stayed one minute longer, she was going to burst into tears and disgrace herself. "*Go.*" She turned on her heel and started back to the house.

"Wait!"

She stopped and looked over her shoulder. "What?"

"I—" His outburst had taken him by surprise. So did his next words. "I'll be back."

She didn't believe him. He was simply trying to smooth over an awkward good-bye. A tourist might say the same thing to the owner of a resort where he had spent a pleasant interlude. She continued walking, and this time she didn't look back.

Nicholas got in the car, backed out of the drive-way, and drove off. And he was nearly at the Oregon-California border before it dawned on him. When he had told her he'd be back, he had been saying he loved her. Only at the time neither of them had realized it.

He hit the steering wheel with his fist. *"Damn!"* What a *fool* he had been!

He almost turned back. Only the thought of Blare kept him heading toward California. But he *would* be back, he thought determinedly.

And this time he would say the words.

Ten

By nine o'clock that morning Angel was high atop
Jane's two-story house, putting on the new roof as
she had promised. She had told Nicholas she
planned to get on with her life, and that was exactly
what she was doing. She laid another shingle and
nailed it into place, using more force than necessary
and receiving great satisfaction in doing so. If Jane
hadn't needed a new roof, she would have had to find
someone who did, she reflected with angry humor.
Damn the man anyway!

He had taken a wrong turn, ended up in her bed,
and then, days later, driven away with her heart.

Well, it didn't matter! She was going to be perfectly fine. And above all, she wasn't going to spend
any time worrying about whether Hawk would
finally succeed in killing him. She really wouldn't,
she told herself, and drove another nail into a
shingle that didn't need it.

• • •

That afternoon Nicholas stood outside the closed office door that was marked simply HAWK. There'd been no need to put Hawk's real name up. Without exception, the service nicknames of himself and his four other friends had stuck with them in civilian life.

He stared at the name, remembering all he and Hawk and the other three had been through together. Hawk had covered his wing on more missions than he could remember and done an excellent job. The five of them had studied together, helping each other make it through flight school. They had danced the night away in Madrid, drunk each other under the table in Saigon, taken turns nursing each other when they had come down with the flu in Cairo.

He could hate Hawk for the danger he had put Angel in. He would also be able to hate him if he had had anything to do with Rocky and Jazz's deaths. But he couldn't hate Hawk for trying to kill him. He couldn't bring himself to believe it was Hawk's fault. It was now apparent that the accident had twisted something in his brain to the point that Hawk was no longer the man he had been.

And Nicholas blamed himself for not seeing it sooner.

If what he suspected was true, Hawk would need confinement and treatment for the rest of his life.

He opened the door and walked in.

Hawk was leaning back in his chair, his feet up on the desk, staring with concentration at the phone. When he looked up and saw Nicholas, the color drained from his face and his feet hit the floor.

"Satan! I was—" He glanced at the phone. "I was just thinking I should be hearing from you."

"Don't you mean you thought that someone from Paradise would be calling here with notification of my death?"

"Why would I think—"

Nicholas's quiet voice cut short his denial. "It was your accident, wasn't it? Somehow you blamed me for it, although I can't for the life of me figure out why."

The tendons on Hawk's arm bulged as he abandoned all pretense of innocence and leaned forward. "*Why*? You don't know *why*? You damned son of a bitch, it was *you* who sent me up on that damned catwalk!"

It was Hawk's face that looked at him, but the man screaming wasn't Hawk, he thought. Still, he couldn't keep himself from trying to reach him. "It was a spur-of-the-moment thing, Hawk, you know that. I know you knew it at the time. Why have you forgotten it? Sending you up there wasn't planned in any way. Why can't you understand?"

"Why would I understand? Why *should* I? You sent *me* up, while you stayed safely on the ground. It wasn't you who had to go through those long months of pain and therapy. It wasn't you who had to learn to cope with the fact that you'd never fly again." His expression suddenly turned sly. "Until recently, that is. I wanted you to know at least part of what I had gone through, and now you do." He laughed, a high-pitched sound. "Just the idea of flying terrifies you."

Nicholas felt immeasurably sad. His old friend had disappeared, and he couldn't reason with this person before him. "What about Rocky and Jazz? Did they fit into your scheme to get back at me?"

A feverish light came into Hawk's eyes. "They were the most important part of my plan. I wanted the satisfaction of seeing you suffer before I killed you, and I decided to use your dream to accomplish it. So I did a little after-hours work on the planes, work that would be destroyed once the planes exploded."

A fierce anger shot through Nicholas. "Jazz and Rocky were not to blame for your accident. How could you have killed them? Dammit, they loved you!"

"I know they did, but more important, *you* loved them. I knew you would die inch by inch thinking that it was your design that had killed them. I planned for Blare to be next, except at Jazz's funeral, I realized I really didn't need for Blare to die. All it had taken was Rocky and Jazz to break you."

If he didn't get out of here soon, Nicholas thought, he was going to throw up. "So you decided I had suffered enough and came after me. Twice."

"Exactly." In his excitement Hawk hit the desk with a closed fist. "It hasn't been as easy to kill you as it was to kill Jazz and Rocky. In fact, I was beginning to think I would have to go on and kill Blare. But it'll be even better now when I finally do kill you, because you'll die knowing the reason." He leaned back in his chair and smiled. "Great plan, don't you think?"

He had heard all he needed to, Nicholas thought tiredly, and there was only one more thing left to do. "Blare."

Stepping into the open doorway, Blare signaled

the three police officers who, along with him, had heard the whole conversation.

With a sigh Angel sat back on her heels and gazed toward the ocean. From Jane's rooftop she had a perfect view. Sunlight danced over the waves, creating a dazzling display of sparkling glints. It was all so beautiful, but she couldn't enjoy it. Though the roof was far from complete, she had already expelled all her energy.

And her anger.

Lord, she hoped Nicholas was all right. But Hawk had proved himself capable of anything, and Nicholas still viewed him as a friend. If Nicholas let his guard down once . . .

She shook her head, trying to rid herself of the frightening images there, but it didn't work. The patrol car parked in Jane's driveway attested to Nicholas's concern for her safety. It seemed to her, therefore, that it was perfectly natural that she should feel some concern for him. It didn't mean that she was pining away for him. Even though she was.

Dammit.

She reached for another shingle and suddenly felt herself lose her balance and pitch forward. Instinctively, she flung out her arm, but there was nothing for her to grab onto but air.

She heard silence and wondered why she wasn't screaming. Even more curious, everything seemed frozen in place but her. She was tumbling down the steep angle of the roof, and she couldn't stop herself, not even at the edge.

For an instant her body was weightless, without

substance, without pain. Then she felt the shock of the impact with the concrete patio.

After that, everything was dark.

"You know, it's the damnedest thing." Blare's tone was weary as he sat slumped in a chair in Nicholas's office. "For most of our adult lives our job was to be ready for war. But there was no way we could have prepared for the war we've just been through, a war in which we lost three of our best friends."

Nicholas, half-lying on a couch not too far from Blare, nodded. "I still can't believe it. It's like some horrible, devastating, completely unthinkable nightmare."

"Or a war."

"Or a war," he said in agreement, reflecting that the two of them were like shell-shock victims. For over a year and without their knowledge, they had most definitely been in a war. He gazed out the window and saw that it was late at night. He wasn't certain of the exact time, and he didn't care. "I kept hoping to see some sign of the old Hawk when they took him away, remorse, something, anything. But there was nothing."

Blare was silent for a moment. "I suppose there is one good thing that has come out of all of this. Lightning One can continue. There's not a thing in the world wrong with your design."

At the moment Nicholas couldn't seem to summon any enthusiasm for the project. All he wanted to do was to go back to Angel, tell her that he loved her, and ask her to forgive him for putting her through such an ordeal.

The phone rang, and Blare reached over to Nicholas's desk and picked up the portable handset. "Santini Aeronautics." He listened, then said, "Yes, just a moment." He leaned forward and extended the phone toward Nicholas. "Someone for you."

He grimaced; he had never felt less like talking to anyone.

With perfect understanding Blare covered the mouthpiece. "Why don't I take a message?"

"All right," he said, but then for some unknown reason, he changed his mind and took the phone. "Hello?"

"Nicholas, it's Jane."

"Jane?" He couldn't imagine why she would be calling him. "How are you?"

"Nicholas, I don't know how to tell you this, or even if I should. I know you're not in love with Angel. . . . I've debated all afternoon about calling you, but I've done it now, and so I'm just going to say it. Angel fell off my roof today. We got her to the hospital as quickly as we could, but"—her voice wavered—"her condition is not good."

"Not good." His brain was slow to comprehend what she was telling him. "But she's going to be all right, isn't she?"

"S-she had a lot of internal injuries, Nicholas. They operated, but—" She began to cry softly. "Matthew's with her now. He says she won't live much longer."

Nicholas sat straight up. "No, that's not right! She's never even been sick!"

"I know, but . . . Everything that can be done has been done."

He surged to his feet. "I'm leaving right now. I'll be there in a few hours."

"Nicholas . . . she doesn't have a few hours."

"What?"

"It won't be much longer. . . ."

He was suddenly cold, as if covered with ice. "I'll be there as fast as I can." He punched the Off button on the phone. "I need a plane, Blare. What do we have available?"

Blare's eyes widened. "You're going to *fly?*"

"I have to. The woman I love is dying."

Without wasting any more time with questions, Blare came to his feet. "Where are you going?"

"Back to Paradise."

"Okay, then I'll check our maps and find out the nearest airport you can land at, then we'll decide on the plane."

Nicholas rubbed his forehead. "Damn! There's not going to be a landing strip anywhere near Paradise that'll take a jet. It's going to have to be a prop. And the only one we have here is yours. Gas it up for me, and I'll get the coordinates."

"That thing won't take you twenty feet!" Blare said with alarm. "The only things holding it together are spit and bailing wire. The reason it's here is because I've been intending to restore it."

"I don't have any choice, Blare."

Blare blew out a long breath. "Okay, I'll gas it up, then after you get in the air, I'll contact the airport to let them know you're coming."

"Also ask them to have a car standing by, plus directions to the hospital. There can't be any delays."

The horror of Angel dying blocked out everything. His whole being was caught up with getting to her. And he was high in the air before the vaguely surprising thought occurred to him that he was flying again, but the thought was fleeting and unimportant to him.

Blare had been right about the condition of the plane, and he had to use all his skill and experience just to keep the plane in the air. The throttle kept getting stuck, and the rudder was stiff and didn't want to work.

He went into an automatic mode. As naturally as if he had been born with the knowledge, he continually adjusted the controls to compensate for not only the throttle and the rudder, but also the fact that the engine was running roughly. At one point the engine stopped completely, but with iron-willed determination and grim perseverance, he got it started again.

Once on the ground, he raced to the waiting car. He scanned the directions, then jammed his foot down on the accelerator and didn't let it up until he had reached the hospital.

"Is she still alive?" Nicholas asked.

"Barely," Matthew said, his face gray with fatigue and sorrow.

"You've got to let me see her."

"I know. Jane and I have already had our time with her." He shook his head, as if there were something very wrong with what he had just said. With tears in his eyes he pointed to the door behind him. "It won't be much longer. Call me. . . . I'll be with Jane in the waiting room."

As fast as he had traveled to get to Angel

Nicholas suddenly felt as if he were moving in slow motion through heavy, dense water. By the time he had reached her bedside, his heart was pounding with the exertion and the grief.

Angel's skin was almost as white as the hospital sheets on which she lay, but even near death, she appeared to be surrounded by radiance. He sank down onto the chair beside the bed and took her hand, careful not to brush any of the tubes connected to her.

One of her arms was in a splint, and the sheet showed an outline of another on her leg. But amazingly he saw no bruises or even a single scratch.

A nearby machine sounded her heartbeat; he listened and willed his to slow so that it would match hers.

"Angel, can you hear me? It's Nicholas. I'm here, and there's something I have to tell you." He searched her face for a sign that she heard him, but her hand remained lifeless in his, and her eyelashes never even fluttered.

"I'm not sure where you are right now, Angel, but I believe with everything that's in me that you can hear me, and I want you to listen carefully. Remember this morning when I told you I'd be back? I could tell that you didn't believe me, and at the time, though I knew it was important I say it, wasn't entirely sure why I did. The truth didn't hit me until after I'd left."

She wasn't responding to him. His chest hurt as if his heart were being squeezed. He brought her hand up to his cheek, trying to warm her skin with his.

"I love you, Angel, and I pray that you believe me. I should have told you this morning. In fact, I should have told you long before I left. I probably fell in love with you the second I opened my eyes and saw this incredibly beautiful angel leaning over me. I looked into those eyes of yours, and I never had a chance." To stem his tears, he chuckled softly. "Oh, I thought I did. I thought I could fight against what I felt for you, but I was deluding myself in a major way. I love you, Angel. And when you get better, you can call me every name in the book for not telling you sooner. But, please, just get better."

Deep sorrow and intense pain had overtaken him. He reached out and stroked her cheek. "Listen to me, I want you to tell your people in heaven they're going to have to wait for you. As a matter of fact, they're going to have to wait a long time. We've got a whole life to live yet. Together. Right here on earth."

His voice broke. "Angel? Please, honey . . . stay with me. You'll never know how much I need you. You fix things. Fix yourself. Dammit, *fix yourself!*

He talked on and on, his voice gradually growing hoarse. At one point Matthew came in to check on her. He didn't say anything, and his expression told Nicholas that he still believed it wouldn't be much longer. But Nicholas could tell that he was surprised Angel was still alive, and he was heartened. As soon as Matthew left, Nicholas started again.

"Did I tell you I flew here? My fear of losing you far outweighed my fear of flying. You fixed me, Angel. Did you hear that? You fixed me. Aft nursing that rattletrap of Blare's all the way here, I'll be able to fly anything. And Lightning One will go on. You were right. My design wasn't at fault. Hawk sabotaged Rocky's and Jazz's planes. But, Angel, the danger is completely over now. If you'll just wake up, I promise you I'll keep you safe for the rest of your life. Angel, I love you so much."

By dawn his voice had almost completely given out, and he was exhausted. Still holding her hand to his cheek, he laid his head down on the bed. Through the night Matthew had continued coming into the room on a regular basis, and each time he had quietly told Nicholas there was no change.

Nicholas's determination that Angel would live had not lessened by even a fraction, but the long hours had taken their toll on him, and he found he couldn't fight off his tears any longer. They slid down his face and spilled onto her hand. "I'm still here, Angel. I'm not going to leave you this time. If you'll stay here with me, I'll never leave you again. I love you. I love you. I love you—"

There was a slight movement against his cheek. At first he thought he had imagined it, but then it happened again. Her fingers were moving!

In one motion he jerked upright, surged to his feet, and bent over her. "Angel? Can you hear me, honey?"

Her lashes fluttered as if she were trying to raise her lids. His weariness and tears vanished. She was trying to come back to him! "I love you, Angel. Open your eyes and look at me, and I promise you, I'll spend the rest of my life convincing you how much I love you."

Her lashes fluttered again, and then slowly her

lids lifted and she was gazing up at him, her eyes a deeper, even more heavenly blue than in the past.

"You're back," he said, breathless with relief.

"You . . . too." Her voice, though weak and whispery, was clear, and he could have shouted for joy.

Instead he grabbed for the call button to summon Matthew.

After Matthew examined Angel and emotionally declared she was out of danger, she closed her eyes once more. But this time Nicholas was assured that she was simply sleeping, not unconscious. He asked that another bed be brought into Angel's hospital room and put beside hers. While she slept, he lay on his side and watched her. Eventually, he was also able to sleep.

But he was awake when she next woke. "Hi there," he said, sitting on the edge of the bed and smiling down at her.

"Hi."

"You gave us all quite a scare, but I knew you would be all right. You had to be. I wouldn't have been able to make it if you hadn't." He paused. "I love you, Angel."

She moistened her lips, then whispered, "I love you too."

Her voice was still weak, but to him her words sounded as if they had been sung by a whole chorus of angels.

"You flew," she murmured.

He started with surprise. "You heard me say that?"

"I don't know. . . . I guess I did."

She had heard him. "Well, I did fly, and under the worse possible circumstances. Wait until you see the junker that brought me here. It was a miracle." He paused, and his tone turned teasing. "Is that why you didn't use your wings to fly when you fell off the roof? Because you wanted me to fly?"

Her mouth quirked.

He smiled. "Uh-huh. I wouldn't put it past you. I'll make you a deal. The next time you want me to do something, just ask."

"You're stubborn. . . ."

"Not anymore. Except about one thing. Angel, will you marry me? You might as well agree, because I won't give up until you do. I refuse to spend one more minute of my life without you. I love you." She smiled, and the smile lighted his heart, his soul, his entire world.

"Yes."

Tears sprang into his eyes, and elation sent his pulses racing out of control. He had made a lot of promises in the night, he thought, and he didn't plan to break one.

Slowly, carefully, he leaned down and pressed a kiss to her mouth. When he had crashed into her life, he had been at the lowest point of his life. Now she was going to be his wife, and someday the mother of his children. And though he was convinced he had cornered all the happiness in the world, he had the strange feeling that their happiness was only just beginning.

Epilogue

Three months later

The rays of the sun reflected off the diamonds in Angel's wedding ring, creating a shower of rainbow sparks as she lifted her hand to shade her eyes. Far out over the desert Lightning One was banking, then angling toward the runway. Nicholas was coming in for a landing after completing an immensely successful test flight.

She supposed it would have been natural if she had been afraid for him and had spent the previous night worrying, but she had slept peacefully, held within the circle of his arms. She had every confidence in both him and his design.

Up in the control tower military officials looked on, but she couldn't have stood to be cooped up inside with a lot of people. Her excitement was too great, her love too overwhelming. She had wanted to be alone, outside, with him.

He was a great pilot, she thought with pride, watching his perfect landing, and he was a great man. His new jet would give future pilots a dimension of safety they had never had before and an advanced technology that would see them well into the twenty-first century.

From her position at the side of the tarmac, she watched his crew rush out to the now-still plane and greet him with whoops of joy as he climbed down from the cockpit.

But within a minute he was striding toward her. She ran to him, and he caught her in his arms and swung her around.

"You were wonderful!" she exclaimed.

He threw back his head and laughed. "It was a piece of cake. My reflexes and skills are sharper than they've ever been before. But then, how could they not be? These days I fly with an angel on my wing."

His mouth came down on hers, and as always, he was swept away by the sweetness and heat.

He had been right about the happiness just beginning, he thought hazily. They had recently bought a new home near his work with acreage that would give Larry, Curly, and Moe plenty of room to run, and the babies that would come room to grow. Although every chance they got, they would return to Paradise, the two of them had created a paradise of their own.

Breaking off the kiss, he drew back and gazed down at her.

His angel.

Her shining blond hair was flying around her head, encircling her with a halo of radiant light, and he saw heaven reflected in the blue of her eyes.

And he wasn't at all surprised when he thought he heard a fluttering of wings in the air around them.

THE EDITOR'S CORNER

As winter's chilly blasts bring a rosy hue to your cheeks and remind you of the approaching holiday season, why not curl up in a cozy blanket with LOVESWEPT's own gift bag of six heartwarming romances.

The ever-popular Helen Mittermeyer leads the list with **KRYSTAL**, LOVESWEPT #516. Krystal Wynter came to Seattle to start over in a town where no one could link her with the scandalous headlines that had shattered her life. But tall, dark, and persistent Cullen Dempsey invades her privacy, claiming her with an intoxicating abandon that awakens old fears and ensnaring her in a web of desire that keeps her from running away. A moving, sensual romance—and another winner from Helen Mittermeyer!

LOVESWEPT's reputation for innovation continues as Terry Lawrence takes you right up to the stars with **EVER SINCE ADAM**, #517, set in an orbiting station in outer space! Maggie Mullins is there to observe maverick astronaut Adam Strade in the environment she helped design—not to succumb to his delicious flirting. And while Adam sweeps her off her feet in zero gravity, he fights letting her get close enough to discover his hidden pain. Don't miss this unique love story. Bravo, Terry, for a romance that's out of this world!

Please give a rousing welcome to Patricia Potter and her first LOVESWEPT, **THE GREATEST GIFT**, #518. Patricia has already garnered popular and critical success with her numerous historical romances, and in **THE GREATEST GIFT** she proves her flair with short, contemporary romance, as well. Writing about a small-town teacher isn't reporter Lane Drury's idea of a dream assignment—until she meets David Farrar. This charming rogue soon convinces her she's captured the most exciting job of all in a romance that will surely be a "keeper." Look for more wonderful stories from Patricia Potter in the year to come.

Let Joan J. Domning engulf you with a wave of passion in **STORMY'S MAN**, LOVESWEPT #519. Gayle Stromm certainly feels as if she's in over her head with Cass Starbaugh, who's six feet six inches of hard muscles, bronzed skin, and sun-streaked hair. Gayle's on vacation to escape nightmares, but caring for the injured mountain climber only makes her dream of a love she thinks she can never have. Cass can't turn down a challenge, though, and he'd do anything to prove to Stormy that she's all the woman he wants. An utterly spellbinding romance by the incomparable Joan J. Domning.

Marvelously talented Maris Soule joins our fold with the stirring **JARED'S LADY**, LOVESWEPT #520. Maris already has several romances to her credit, and you'll soon see why we're absolutely thrilled to have her. Jared North can't believe that petite Laurie Crawford is the ace tracker the police sent to find his missing niece, and, to Laurie's dismay, he insists on joining the search. She's had enough of overprotective men to last a lifetime, yet raw hunger sparks inside her at his touch. Together these two create an elemental force that will leave you breathless and looking for the next LOVESWEPT by Maris Soule.

IRRESISTIBLE, LOVESWEPT #521 by beloved author Joan Elliot Pickart, is the perfect description for Pierce Anderson. This drop-dead-gorgeous architect thinks he's hallucinating when a woman-sized chicken begs him to unzip her. But when a dream girl emerges from the feathers, he knows the fever he feels has nothing to do with the flu! Calico Smith struggles to resist the sensual power of Pierce's kissable lips. She's worked so hard for everything she has, while he's never fought for what he wanted—until now. Another fabulous romance from Joan Elliott Pickart.

And (as if these six books aren't enough) LOVESWEPT is celebrating the joyous ritual of weddings with a contest for you, a contest that will have three winners! Look for details in the January 1992 LOVESWEPTS.

Don't forget FANFARE, where you can expect three superb books this month. **THE FLAMES OF VENGEANCE** is the second book in bestselling Beverly Byrne's powerful trilogy. From rebellion plotted beneath cold, starry skies to the dark magic that stalks the sultry Caribbean night, Lila Curran's web, baited with lust and passion, is carefully being spun. Award-winning Francine Rivers delivers a compelling historical romance in **REDEEMING LOVE**. Sold into sin as a child, beautiful, tormented "Angel" never believed in love until the strong and tender Michael Hosea walked into her life. Can their radiant happiness conquer the darkest demons from her past? Much-acclaimed Sandra Brown will find a place in your heart—if she hasn't already—with **22 INDIGO PLACE**. Rebel millionaire James Paden has a dream—to claim 22 Indigo Place and its alluring owner, Laura Nolan, the rich man's daughter for whom he'd never been good enough. Three terrific books from FANFARE, where you'll find only the best in women's fiction.

As always at this season, we send you the same wishes. May your New Year be filled with all the best things in life—the company of good friends and family, peace and prosperity, and, of course, love.

Warm wishes from all of us at LOVESWEPT and FANFARE,

Nita Taublib

Nita Taublib
Associate Publisher, LOVESWEPT
Publishing Associate, FANFARE

conceals. No one knows of her secret alliance, her mysterious lover, or her raging obsession to control the House of Mendoza.

From the bloody streets of Dublin to London's exquisite drawing rooms to the dark magic of the Caribbean, the Black Widow's web, baited with lust and passion, is carefully being spun. . . .

The following excerpt begins the novel. All copy must be double spaced. Fill boxes from edge to edge.

Prologue

Cordoba, Spain

1860 The darkness moved and breathed as if alive. It defined everything in Lila Curran's world. She lived in perpetual night, the details of her captivity conveyed to her by all her senses except sight. Sound snaked through her black shroud, twisted around her, strangled her will to resist. The metal collar around her neck was heavy, the marble floor cold, and the woven carpet she lay on rough. The sides of the enormous carved wooden bed to which she was chained were high, and the bed itself an almost unendurable torment–it was placed just inches too far for her to climb on.

Lila could hear her child crying. Her six month old son was in the room adjacent to hers. He'd been christened Miguel in the Spanish fashion, but to her–always–he was Michael. Her baby boy, the sweet tender infant born, she'd thought, of love and trust, had become as much an object of his father's hatred as she. Twice a day a wetnurse came and fed him and attended to his needs, the rest of the time Michael was alone and frightened, and he wept. And Lila tore at her chains and screamed out her fury and her pain. But no one dared admit they heard.

Around her and Michael the household in the ancient and venerable Palacio Mendoza kept to its ordinary daily routine. Lila heard through her darkness the noises of servants going about their chores, of her husband, the mighty Juan Luis Mendoza, stomping along the passage outside her door or venting his insane rages in the patio below her balcony. Occasionally she heard the voice of Juan Luis's sister Beatríz or of her husband Francisco. Her in-laws knew she was a captive.

But they, too, were Juan Luis's prisoners, incapable of breaking the bonds of his tyrannical rule—in thrall to the Mendoza legacy of power and wealth.

1861.

They brought her food once a day, always the same, a kind of stew of vegetables and a bit of meat in a wooden bowl. No spoon was provided, to survive she must bury her face in the dish like an animal. Lila did it, she did whatever was necessary, because one thing she had determined in the thirteen months since Juan Luis had chained her. She would survive and she would be avenged.

Until the day when the voice of the child was silenced.

Lila listened for him, her heartbeats timed to his cries as they had been since her torment began, but there was nothing. She had thought there was no terror or fury she had not already plumbed, but the knowledge that Michael was gone—dead? murdered by his own father?—was a visitation from hell. Her pain and rage were beyond imagining. She could not scream, she hadn't the strength. All she could do was lay on the floor, her hands clasped to the metal collar around her neck.

Hours passed. And then she knew. Juan Luis had won. She was at last the victim of total despair.

"Lila, Lila, *¿puedes escucha me, mi niña?*" The voice seemed to come from far away. It repeated the question a second time, in labored English, an urgent whisper. "Can you hear me? It is I, your sister-in-law, Beatriz. Lila, in God's name, are you alive?"

Her name, spoken in a human voice. In all the long days and weeks and months of her agony, she had not heard her name, the acknowledgment of her existence as a separate human being. "I . . . I am alive." Her lips cracked and began to bleed with the effort of making words. "Beatriz, my baby, my Michael—"

"Ssh, do not talk, only listen. I am outside the door, I bribed a maid to unlock the corridor, but she would not dare to give me the key to this room. Juan Luis has terrified her, terrified all the servants. Beatriz's voice broke. "Terrified even us."

"Michael," Lila whispered. "My Michael . . ."

"That is what I have come to tell you. He is all right, *mi niña*, he is with me. Francisco and I have taken him to our apartments. I could live with it no longer, this wickedness. I prayed. I gathered courage. Then I told my crazy brother that if he did not give me the baby to look after I would make a scandal, even he could not survive. To torture a helpless infant, it is unthinkable. All Andalusia would treat him as a leper . . . Lila, do you understand? Your little Miguel, he is fine. He will be well, I will take care of him until Juan Luis comes to his senses." There was no reply. "Lila," Beatriz called again, "Lila, ¿puedes escucha me?"

The whispered response came after some seconds. "Sí, escucho yo. I hear you, I understand."

Her child was alive, well, cared for. It gave her courage. Lila knew she would survive.

1872. Sometimes Michael came to the balcony of her room. It was a difficult trick, he had to be quite certain that neither his father nor any of his father's spies would see him, he had to hoist himself up to the second story using only the vines which grew on the stone walls of the palace as handholds, but he managed to do it sometimes.

Lila had been torn apart when the clandestine visits began. She longed to see her son, but she hated for him to see her. True, things were somewhat better now after three years. The metal collar and the chains had been removed, a gesture of munificence on the part of Juan Luis, some kind of relenting of his mad, unfounded jealously, but she was still a prisoner in this single room. Her hair, once flaming red, had turned to silver, she was as thin as a wraith—a shadow who dwelled among shadows, not a woman.

"Mama! Mama, are you there?" The boy pressed his face to the glass of the balcony doors. They were locked and he had never managed to find a key that would open them, but when his mother heard his voice she usually came and parted the draperies a crack, they could peer at each other through the opening, separated, unable to touch, but with an illusion of closeness. "Mama," the boy called again. "Please answer me, it's important."

The curtains parted—only a hair, to open them wider might alert watching eyes, it was far too dangerous. "I'm here, darling. How are you?"

"I'm fine, Mama, fine."

Lila filled her being with the sight of him. He was a big child, enormous for thirteen, with her red hair and vivid blue eyes darker than hers. She pressed her fingertips to the glass. If only she could touch his face. Michael . . . Michael . . . the child of her agony, of her heart, the son she had not embraced since he was three months old. "Michael," she whispered, her mouth hovering near the panes as if her breath might kiss him though her lips could not.

"Mama, listen, I have something for you. It was wonderful luck that Tia Beatriz and I saw this letter before Papa did. She said I should bring it to you."

Lila looked at the envelope, it was large and thick. She had no idea where it had come from or how she could hope to put her hands on it. It was too fat for Michael to slide between the cracks. "Michael, you cannot give it to me. It won't fit. Besides, it's too dangerous. If your father finds out–"

"I don't care," the boy said. "It's important, I know it is. I'm going to break the glass." He held up something else. A large stone.

"Michael! No, you mustn't. Your father–"

"I don't care! I'm going to break the glass and get you out. We will run away from the Palacio Mendoza. We will run so far that Papa will never find us."

There was no place on this earth beyond the grasp of the enormous wealth and power of the Mendozas, Lila knew it, even if her son didn't. Besides, she had no money, no family, nothing. Where could she take him? What would they do? "No," she whispered. "No."

"Mama, the letter is important. I know it is. I feel in my bones that it is."

Lila looked at the envelope. She felt something too. Something indescribable, something she had long ago thought was dead in her. Courage, the ability to do more than merely survive, a freshening of her will to triumph. She reached out a hand as if to take the document. It drew her with a mysterious power, a sense of absolute rightness, of destiny. "Yes," she whispered. "Yes, Michael, do it. Break the glass. Only enough to get the letter in, only one pane. I can cover the break so it won't be discovered for a while."

Juan Luis came to her that night. He often came these days. He would pace up and down the room which was her prison and rave at her, tell her of her crimes, of how she had cuckolded him. She'd long ago given up remonstrating, no arguments of hers could alter his insane fixation on imagined betrayals. Her only reply was silence. Tonight she listened for long minutes, aware of the stirring of air in the room from the broken glass as yet unnoticed. The letter weighed ominously heavy in the pocket of her gown. Finally she did what she had not done in months, she spoke.

"Juan Luis, listen to me."

He froze, startled by the voice he had not heard for so long. "So you deign to answer? To what do I owe the honor?"

"To the truth, Juan Luis. To knowledge. I have knowledge, and because of it you are going to set me free. Me and my son."

"What are you talking about?"

"Power," Lila said softly. "I am talking about power. And you are going to listen."

Two days after the letter was placed in Lila Curran's hands she and her son Michael left the Palacio Mendoza. Their journey took mere weeks, but their odyssey would take many years and span two continents. They had embarked on a quest for that most elusive of all rewards; they wanted reparation for the lost years, the countless humiliations. They craved vengeance.

*   *   *   *   *

R E D E E M I N G   L O V E
By Francine Rivers
author of REBEL IN HIS ARMS

From Francine Rivers comes a romance of redemptive love . . . sold into sin as a child, beautiful, tormented Angel never believed in love until the strong and tender Michael Hosea walked into her life. Pursued by this young man's unconditional love, Angel discovers a sweet vulnerability she's never known—until her new life is threatened by the darkest demons of her past. Can she conquer her difficult destiny and keep the man she now adores

In this opening scene from REDEEMING LOVE, we see the struggle between good and evil . . .

The prince of darkness is a gentleman.
                    Shakespeare
New England, 1837

Alex Stafford was just like Mama had said. He was tall and dark and Sarah had never seen anyone so beautiful. Even dressed in dusty riding clothes, his hair damp with perspiration, he was like the princes in the stories Mama read. Sarah's heart beat with wild joy and pride. None of the other fathers she saw at Mass compared to him.

He looked at her with his dark eyes and her heart sang. She was wearing her best blue frock and white pinafore, and Mama had braided her hair with pink and blue ribbons. Did Papa like the way she looked? Mama said blue was his favorite color, but why didn't he smile? Was she fidgeting? Mama said to stand straight and still and act like a lady. He would like that. But he didn't look pleased at all.

"Isn't she beautiful, Alex?" Mama said, her voice oddly constricted. "Isn't she the most beautiful little girl you've ever seen?"

Alex saw the hope in his mistress' eyes and frowned darkly. He was tired of being pressed from all directions. He had ridden four hours to get here and he had but two to stay. He wanted Mae in bed, warm and willing. He didn't want to waste time on a child, even one of his own breeding, rotten luck that it was.

"Just a few minutes," Mae said, seeing his impatience, afraid Sarah would as well. "That's all I'm asking, Alex. Please."

He studied the little girl. She had his chin and nose, but otherwise he saw little of himself in her. She was blond and fair like her mother, although her eyes were a more vivid blue. She was pretty, almost too pretty, and she gazed up at him as though he were God Himself. She made him damned uncomfortable. Why had Mae done it? Hadn't he made it clear enough?

"Did you pick blue on purpose, Mae?" he said, unable to keep the cold rage from his tone. "Because it brings out the color of her eyes?"

His mockery cut her like a slashing blade. It was the side of

Alex she feared most, his brutal sarcasm, words far more cruel than a slap across her face.

Alex glanced toward the foyer. "Cleo!"

"She's not here," Mae said quietly. "I gave her the day off."

"Did you?" he said. "Well, that leaves you in a bit of a fix, doesn't it?"

Mae stiffened. She could see plainly he had not the least intention of spending even a moment with Sarah. How could he be so heartless? Was he blind to the adoration in his child's eyes? "What would you have me do?"

His dark eyes glinted. "Send her away. She knows how to find Cleo, I'd imagine."

Sarah's smile fell in confusion. They spoke so coldly to one another. Neither looked at her. Had they forgotten she was there? What was wrong? Mama was distraught. Why was Papa so angry about Cleo not being here?

Chewing on her lip, Sarah looked between them and tugged on her father's jacket. "Papa . . ."

"Don't call me that," he said tersely.

She blinked, frightened and confused. He *was* her Papa. Mama said so. He even brought her presents every time he came. Mama gave them to her. "You bring me presents. . . ."

"Hush, Sarah. Not now, darling," Mae said quickly.

Papa flashed Mama a thunderous look. "Let her speak. It's what you wanted, isn't it? Why are you afraid now, Mae?" Mama touched her shoulder with trembling fingers, but Papa bent toward her, smiling now though his eyes glittered strangely. He took her hand and she trembled with happiness. "What presents?" he asked.

He was so beautiful and she loved him so much she could not speak. "Tell me, little one."

"I . . . I always like the candles you bring me," Sarah said, glowing beneath his attention. "But best of everything, I love the crystal swan."

Afraid, Mae put a trembling hand to her throat. Alex would never understand. His face darkened and his eyes became like steel shards. "Indeed," he said and straightened. He looked at Mama again. "I'm pleased to know that."

Sarah looked up at her father. But if he said he was, then he must be. She rushed on brightly, "I put it on my window sill. The sun shines through it and makes colors dance on the wall. Would you like to come and see?" She took his hand, frowning when he pulled his away.

Mae bit her lip and gave him a pleading look, but she saw he was coldly furious.

Alex wanted to strike her. Was that all his gifts had meant to her? Trinkets to be tossed away on a child? And what about his love? She had given that to the child also.

Mae could not bear the coldness in his expression and lowered her eyes. "Darling, be a good girl and go outside and play."

Sarah looked up, distressed. "Can't I stay? I'll be very quiet." Mama couldn't seem to say more. Her eyes were moist and she looked at Papa.

Alex bent down. "I want you to go outside and play," he told her. "I want to talk to your mother alone."

"Can I come back?" Sarah asked hopefully.

"Your mother will come and get you when she's ready. Now, run along as you've been told."

Sarah wanted to stay, but she wanted to please her father more. She went out of the parlor, skipping through the kitchen to the back door. She picked a few daisies that grew in the garden patch by the door and headed for the rose lattice. She plucked the petals, "He loves me, he loves me not, he loves me, he loves me not. . . ." She hushed as she came around the corner. She did not want to disturb Mama and Papa.

The parlor window was open there. Sarah wanted to sit and be close to her parents, and know just when Papa wanted her to come back again. If she was quiet, she wouldn't disturb them, and all Mama would have to do is lean out and call her.

"What was I to do?" Mama cried out. "You've never spent so much as a minute with her. What was I to tell her, Alex? That her father doesn't care? That he wished she had never even been born?"

Sarah's lips parted. Deny it, Papa! Deny it!

"I brought that swan back from Europe for you, and you throw it away on a child. Did you give her the pearls as well? What about the music box? I suppose she got that, too."

Sarah blinked. The daisies fell from her hand and she sat down on the ground, careless of her pretty dress. Her heart slowed from its wild, happy beat. Everything inside her seemed to spiral downward.

"Alex, please," Mama pledged. "I didn't see any harm in it.

It made it easier. She asked me this morning if she was old enough to meet you. She asks me every time she knows you're coming. How could I say no? I didn't have the heart. She doesn't understand your neglect and neither do I."

"You know how I feel about her," Alex said.

"How can you say how you feel? You don't even know her. She's a beautiful child, Alex. She's quick and charming and she isn't afraid of anything. She's like you in so many ways. She's someone, Alex. You can't ignore her existence forever. She's your daughter."

"I have enough children by my wife. I told you I didn't want or need another one."

"How can you say that?" Mae cried. "How can you not love your own flesh and blood?"

"I told you how I felt from the beginning, but you wouldn't listen. She should never have been born, but you insisted on having your own way."

"Do you think I wanted to get pregnant?" Mae cried angrily. "Do you think I planned to have her?"

"I've often wondered. Especially when I arranged a way out of the situation for you and you refused. The doctor I sent to you would have taken care of the whole mess. He would've gotten rid—"

"I couldn't do it," she said. "How could you expect me to kill my unborn child? Don't you understand? It's a mortal sin."

"You've spent too much time in church," he said derisively. "Have you ever thought that you wouldn't have the problems you do now if you had gotten rid of her? It would have been easy. But you ran out."

"I wanted her," Mama said brokenly. "She was part of you, Alex, and part of me. I wanted her even if you didn't."

"Is that the real reason?"

Mama gasped. "You're hurting me. . . ."

Sarah flinched as something shattered. "Is that the real reason, Mae? Or did you have her because you thought bearing my child would give you a hold over me you otherwise lacked?"

"You can't believe that!" She was crying. "But you do, don't you? You're a fool. Mother of God, and I gave up everything for you. My family, my friends, my self-respect, everything I believed in, every hope I ever had. . . ."

"I bought you this cottage. I give you all the money you could possibly need. . . ."

Mama's voice rose strangely. "Do you know what's it's like for me to walk down the street in this town? You come and go when and as you please. And they know who you are and they know what I am. No one looks at me, Alex. No one speaks to me. Sarah feels it, too. She asked me about it once and I told her we were invisible. I didn't know what else to say," she cried out, her voice breaking. "I'll probably go to hell for what I've become."

"I'm sick of your guilt and I'm sick of hearing about that child. She's ruining everything between us. Do you remember how happy we were? We never argued. I couldn't wait to come to you, and I couldn't get enough of you when I did."

"Don't . . ."

"Your body still shakes when I hold you like this. And how much time have I left with you today? Enough? You've used it up on her. I told you what would happen. Didn't I? I wish she had never been born!"

"Sarah. Her name is Sarah. Sarah!"

"Sarah be damned."

"You bastard!"

Mama cried out in pain. "Bastard," she screamed. "Bastard, bastard!" There was a crash. Terrified, Sarah got up and ran. She raced through Mama's flowers and across the lawn and onto the pathway to the springhouse. She ran until she couldn't run anymore. Gasping, with her sides burning, she dropped into the tall grass, her shoulders heaving with sobs, her face streaked with tears. She heard a horse galloping toward her. She scrambled for a better hiding place in the vines about the creek. Peering out, she saw her father ride by on his great black horse. Ducking down, she huddled there, crying, and waited for Mama to come for her.

But Mama didn't come and she didn't call for her. After a while, Sarah wandered back to the springhouse and sat by the flowered vines and waited longer. By the time Mama came, Sarah had dried her tears and dusted off her pretty frock. She was shaking from what she had heard.

Mama was very pale, her eyes dull and red-rimmed. There was a blue mark on the side of her face. She had tried to cover it with powder. She smiled, but it wasn't like her usual smile. "Where have you been, darling? I've been looking and looking for you." But Sarah knew she hadn't. Sarah had been watching for *her*. Mama licked her lacy handkerchief and wiped a smudge from Sarah's cheek. "Your father was called away suddenly on business."

"Is he coming back?" Sarah asked, afraid. She never wanted to see him again. He had hurt Mama and made her cry.

Mae saw the tears in her daughter's eyes. "Maybe not for a long time. We'll have to just wait and see. He's a very busy and important man." She had never seen Alex so angry, not even when she had refused to have the abortion. He had bought the cottage and then left her, not returning until six weeks after Sarah was born. She didn't know if he would ever return now, not after the things she had said. And he had struck her twice and looked at her afterward as though he hated the very sight of her.

She had so hoped to touch the gentler side of him, the side she knew so well. Instead, she had roused a devil.

Why hadn't she left well enough alone?

What was she to do if he didn't come back?

She couldn't let herself think about it or she would cry and frighten Sarah. Thank God, Alex had enough sensitivity to send Sarah from the room before unleashing his temper. What if Sarah had heard all those horrible things? Thank God she had gone out to play before Alex's temper had erupted and her own sense had blown away before the storm of his rage.

"It's all right, sweetheart," Mae said, lifting her and hugging her close. "You know what we're going to do? We're going to go back to the cottage and change our dresses. Then we'll pack a picnic and go down to the creek. Would you like that?"

Sarah nodded and put her arms around Mama's neck. Her mouth trembled and she tried not to cry. If she cried, Mama might guess she had been eavesdropping and then she would be angry, too.

Mae held her tightly, her face buried in Sarah's hair. She smelled so good. She could hold her child like this forever. "We'll make it through this. You'll see," she whispered. "We will. *We will.*"

＊   ＊   ＊   ＊   ＊

New York *Times* bestselling author
Sandra Brown's

2 2   I N D I G O   P L A C E

*Once James Paden had been the high-school bad boy—too
dangerous to flirt with, but too gorgeous to ignore! Now Laura
Nolan faced him as a woman, about to lose the home that had
been a symbol of the good life in her small town to a man whose
desire for her—and for 22 Indigo Place—had only deepened over
time. What gave this man the devastating power to seduce her
senses, to make her shiver with emotions she dared not confess? In
his mind she'd always been the girl he couldn't have, the rich
man's daughter for whom he'd never be good enough . . . until
that moonlit night when the fierce touch of his lips branded her
forever his.*

*In this scene, inside 22 Indigo Place, James and Laura have just
met again after his long absence from town. . . .*

"You haven't changed, Laura."

"His use of her first name alone caused goose bumps to break
out on her arms. No longer mocking, his voice was soft and
raspy, the way she remembered it sounding when they had met
on the street and he had spoken to her. She had always spoken
back courteously, ducking her head modestly and hurrying on
her way, in case anybody watching mistook her friendliness as a
come-on.

For some reason, exchanging hellos with James Paden had
always left her a trifle breathless and disconcerted. She had felt
compromised just by his speaking her name, as though he had
touched her instead. Maybe because his eyes *implied* more than
a simple hello. But for whatever reason, she had always been
affected.

She felt that same way now. Awkward. Tongue-tied. And
guilty over nothing. "I'm older."

"You're better looking."

"Thank you." She knotted her fingers together in her lap. Her palms were so sweaty, they made a damp spot on her skirt.

"Everything's still firm and compact." His eyes scaled down her with the practiced ease of a man who is accustomed to mentally undressing women. When he raised his eyes to her face again, he looked at her from beneath a shelf of brows.

"I try to watch my weight." She was uneasy at being scrutinized with such blatant sexual interest, but she couldn't quite bring herself to admonish him for it. It was safer to pretend she didn't notice.

"Your hair still looks shiny and soft. Remember when I told you it was the color of a fawn?" Lying, she shook her head.

"You dropped your chemistry book in the hallway, and I picked it up for you. Your hair swung down across your cheek. That's when I told you it looked like a fawn."

It had been her algebra book and they were in the school cafeteria, not the hallway. She said nothing.

"It's still that same, soft color. And it still has those blond streaks around your face. Or do you have those put there now?"

"No, they're natural."

He smiled at her sudden response. Laura had the grace to smile back shyly. He stared at her for a long time. "As I said, you're the prettiest girl in town."

"The prettiest *rich* girl."

He shrugged. "Hell, everybody was rich compared to the Padens."

Laura glanced down at her hands, embarrassed for him. James had grown up on the wrong side of the tracks, literally. He had lived in a shack held together by whatever scrap materials his alcoholic father could salvage from the junkyard. From the outside the tiny house had looked like a patchwork quilt, a laughable eyesore. Laura had often wondered how James had managed to keep himself clean, living in that shack.

"I was sorry about your father," she said quietly. Old Hector Paden had died several years ago. His death went virtually unnoticed, certainly unlamented.

James laughed scoffingly. "Then you were the only one."

"How's your mother?"

He stood up suddenly, his body tense. "She's all right, guess."

Laura was stunned by his apparent indifference. While James was growing up, Leona Paden had held countless jobs to support her son and husband. But because of chronic absenteeism and illness, she earned the reputation of being unreliable. Shortly after her husband's death, however, she had moved from the shack by the railroad tracks into a small, neat house in a respectable neighborhood. Laura rarely saw Mrs. Paden anymore. She kept to herself. It was rumored that James supported her, so it came as a shock to Laura now that he would dismiss his mother with an uncaring shrug.

He went around the room, picking up an object and examining it carefully before setting it down and going to the next. "Why are you selling the place?"

Laura didn't like feeling that he was a prosecutor cross-examining her, so she stood up, too, and wen to the window with the hope that she would see Mrs. Hightower's car coming up the lane. "Father died last February, so I live here alone. It's ridiculous for one person to live in a house this large."

He watched her intently. She was careful to keep her expression inscrutable. "Before his death, only you and your father lived here?"

"Yes. Mother died a few years ago." She averted her eyes. "Of course Bo and Gladys Burton lived in the quarters," she added, referring to the couple who had worked as domestics for her family for as long as she could remember.

"They don't anymore?"

"No, I let them go."

"Why?"

Feeling trapped, she moved away from him. "I've heard about your success with those . . . those . . ."

"Automotive-parts stores."

"I was very glad for you."

He laughed shortly, scornfully. "Yeah, I'm sure everybody in town has toasted my success. They were so sure when I left here ten years ago that I'd be in prison by now."

"Well, what did you expect everybody to think? The way you—Never mind."

"No, go on," he said, stepping around in front of her again. "Tell me. The way I what?"

"The way you caroused in those cars you were always tinkering with."

"I worked in a garage. Tinkering with cars was how I made my living."

"But you delighted in scaring other drivers by whipping in and out of traffic with your hot rods and motorcycles. That's how you got your kicks. Just like tonight!" she said, pointing toward the lawn through the wide, tall windows. "Why were you hiding there in the bushes just waiting to scare me to death?"

He grinned. "I wasn't waiting for you. I was waiting for Mrs. Hightower."

"Well, you would have scared her too. Looming out of the dark on that horrible, noisy thing. She would have fainted. You should be ashamed of yourself."

He leaned down, laughing softly. "You can still get mad as the dickens, can't you Laura?"

She drew herself up. "I'm extremely even-tempered."

He laughed again. "I remember when you lit into Joe Don Perkins for knocking over your cherry Coke at the soda fountain in the drugstore. A bunch of us had gone in there to buy . . . uh . . . never mind what we were buying, but I'll never forget how Joe Don tucked in his tail and slunk out of the drugstore after you let him have it with both barrels. You called him a big, clumsy oaf."

James was bending over her now, having backed her against the windowsill. He reached up and playfully tugged on a strand of light blond hair that lay against her cheek, then rested his palm there. "I remember thinking how damned exciting you were when you got mad." His voice dropped. "You're still exciting." He stroked her cheek.

FANFARE

Now On Sale
THE FLAMES OF VENGEANCE